SCEPTER OF FIRE

VIGILANT ◆ BOOK 2

BY

L.M. PRESTON

CONTENTS

COPYRIGHTS

Reproducing this book without permission from the author or the publisher is an infringement of its copyright. This book is a work of fiction. The names characters, places, and incidents are products of the author's imagination and are not to be construed as real. No part of this book may be used or reproduced in any manner whatsoever without permission, except in the case of brief quotations embodied in critical articles and reviews.

Copyright © 2020 by LM Preston.
All rights reserved.
ISBN: 978-1-7329247-5-8

Editor: Cindy Davis
Proof Reader: Dawn Yacovetta
Cover Design by We've Got You Covered. All Rights Reserved.
Interior Design and Formatting by Stephany Wallace @S.W. Creative Publishing co All Rights Reserved.

A Phenomenal One Press publication, May 2020
www.phenomenalonepress.com

SYPNOSIS

Scepter of Fire –Book 2: Vigilant Series

Dexter didn't like being a pawn. It seemed life was taking him there though. He and his father never saw eye to eye, but being captured and tortured for his father's mistakes gave Dexter too much to think about. First, the girl he lost; he'd never forget what they did to her. It changed him and made him see the small city where his father moved him was a prison for magicals, the damned, and now him. Too bad the creator of the Void didn't realize they would be better off if they'd set him free because now he was fighting for his life, along with someone he'd have to hide his feelings from to protect, not just from those who want to drag them back but from himself—a Vigilant.

visit www.lmpreston.com/store

ALSO BY L.M. PRESTON

PURGATORY REIGN SERIES

Purgatory Reign, Book 1

Deviant Storm, Book 2

Colliding Souls

Fierce Tides, Book 3

THE PACK SERIES

The Pack, Book 1

Retribution, Book 2

THE BANDITS SERIES

Bandits, Book 1

Wastelands, Book 2

Double Trouble Luv

Thundering Luv

Flutter of Luv

VIGILANT SERIES

Insatiable Darkness, Book 0.

Caged Fire, Book 1.

Unbreakable Darkness, Book 1.5

STANDALONES

Flutter Of Luv

Thundering Luv

Double Trouble Luv

NON FICTION

Building Your Empowered Steps

Homeschooling and Working While

Raising Amazing Learners

Team Wave Surfing

ACKNOWLEDGMENTS

Thanks to God for giving me this anxious energy to create and tenacious spirit of positivity with an active imagination. To my devoted Beta Reader, my daughter, and Proof Reader, Dawn. To my editor, Cindy Davis, who's been my best support in my art.

DEDICATION

This series is dedicated to my four kids. You each have your own superpowers within you. We are all survivors and have been through some awesome adventures together. They fuel my characters and give me endless material. You are a major encouragement to keep writing, and I couldn't ask for a better support team for allowing me to read my stories to you, asking you for names of my characters, or to show me martial arts moves while staging live-action sparring exercises. To my husband who keeps pushing me to be more creative and makes sure I don't give up.

Dex kept his eyes closed. The bindings at his wrists were cold, unforgiving chains. He needed to stay calm, take it all in, and wait until they'd left him alone. His shirt was loose. His sleeve covered one of the chains on his wrist while the other was rolled high on his shoulder.

"Doctor Rutherford said to hold the patient down until they come to take him," mentioned a woman who adjusted his head on the pillow.

"How long has he been like that?" a male asked.

Dex remained stone still, keeping his breathing even as his nose nearly twitched from the man's breath near his face. He felt the lift of his eyelid. Concentrating on keeping extremely still while the man flashed a light into them was nearly impossible. Dex forced his eyes not to focus but noted the man's dark skin and brown eyes. He could have sworn the guy winked at him. Still, Dex didn't trust it; he didn't budge. The man let go of Dex's eyelid. Dex almost sighed. It was hard to not blink. He had to wait, though, for that one chance to escape.

"This isn't a game. I've witnessed enough in this hospital to know. Mind your business and stay out of the wa..." the woman warned.

Dex forced his fist not to clench at the mention of his family who was in the car crash with him. He remembered when they sank into the water. He'd fought to get the door open and his younger siblings out of the vehicle. Then, something hit his head, and everything went dark.

"Like you, I just work here for the paycheck. I was assigned to the ER when they brought the family in to be treated. I wanted to see how he was doing myself. I swear he wasn't breathing when they pumped his stomach of lake water."

"Nathan," she shushed him, "give him the shot and clear out. You don't want to be here when they take them. It's never pleasant." She cleared her throat. "You're new here, and if you want to keep your job, you will stop asking questions."

"I am trying to help."

"The men coming to get him are not to be trifled with—" She exhaled a shaky sigh—"I don't even think they are human. Stay out of their way, and you won't become a casualty of this patient's transfer."

Click clack click. Light, and sure footsteps; he could tell it was the female nurse. Nathan remained there, though. The guy stood still, but the heaviness of his presence was over him. Dex felt the presence of the woman leave the room. The door closed.

"I can't help you much, but if you have it in you, get the hell out of here. The hospital is going up in flames. Your father and oldest sister are on this floor, the others... Sorry, we couldn't help all of you."

Dex didn't trust the man. He remained still as the chains on his feet were removed.

"Damn! They didn't give me the keys for your wrists. Sorry kid." Nathan messed with the screws on the sides of the bed. "That's the best I can do. The camera is dead. Do what you got to do to break those chains. And forget my name."

Heavy footsteps left the room. The door closed.

Grunting, Dex opened his eyes to the dim hospital room. The dripping IV on his arm wasn't doing a good enough job at keeping him asleep. He was a Vigilant now – human, but with something else: a gift, a curse, he didn't know yet. His father never had the chance to tell him before their escape from the Void went bad. With a hard pull, the chains fell away from Dex's wrists. He ripped the IV from his arm and got out of the bed. He searched around the room for his shoes. Damn, he wanted the new pair of designer tennis shoes his mother bought him. He'd need them for where he was going, which was far away from the hospital.

He scanned the room until his eyes landed on them. His heart pumped rapidly in his chest, but he wasn't leaving without his shoes. The last thing his mom gave him. He forced his breathing to slow then stuffed his feet into them. Dex leaned against the door, bearing down on it so no one could walk in on him. Shoes tied; he snatched the chains off the bed. Chains they'd used to hold him down in case he woke up from his fake coma. Chains he'd wrap around the neck of anyone who would try to hurt him or his family again. He stuffed them in his pocket to mute the jingling.

Slowly, Dex cracked open the door. A bead of sweat slid down the side of his face. Dex wiped it away. He rubbed his hand into his mass of curly, tapered hair and peered through the crack he'd made in the door. The hall was clear; he slid from the room, closing it back before crouching low. The hall was dim. The hospital smelled of antiseptic and sickness. The walls were stained and cracked. Dex frowned, the hallways were dingy, but his room was modern and immaculate.

The sound of voices teased the hall. Dex crept to the side

of the large nurse's desk. He crouched lower and held his breath.

"Check the room. Jake and his team got the others on the bottom floor."

"The sister up here?" called another man.

"She's at the end of the corridor. We'll get her after the boy Dexter...the other, Lewis, isn't going anywhere." The guy laughed.

"Hey Coach Moreau; he's not in there," a younger male voice said.

"What the hell you say?"

Dex frowned. He didn't know why the head coach Moreau was looking for him. The man was a Soul Thief, and Dex knew from experience none of them were any good. Moreau couldn't know about the Soul Thief ring he'd taken from Grady's dead body. No one knew except his father.

Dex peeked around the desk. There were five of them. All grown men except one guy he'd seen on the varsity football team who had graduated this year. He slowly exhaled. He had to get to his oldest sister, EmVee, before they did.

He glanced at the window; it was a long way down. The moon was high but bright in the sky.

The men cursed and ran down the opposite hall. Dex figured they were going to find the nurses. He made his move and slowly stood. The hallway was clear. He jogged on light feet to the end of the hall.

"Hey! There, get him," someone called after him.

Dex picked up speed and rounded the corner. A doctor rushed out of a room at the end of the hall then took off running in the opposite direction. Dex slid to a halt. Kayson, from his football team, came out of a room ahead. It had to be his sister's room. Kayson was a friend of hers. He pulled her from the water.

He ran up to Kayson and pushed him back into the room. "They are after me. You got to get my sister out of here."

Kayson seemed confused. "How the hell am I supposed to do that?"

"Do it! I will cause a commotion. Just get her out of here."

"Fine." Kayson went over to EmVee who was groggy, but at Kayson's whispered demand, she grasped Kayson's shirt.

Dex took a deep breath, sniffed back a tear, hoping he would be able to meet them later—somewhere, anywhere but in this hospital.

"The window, it's the only way." Dex opened the door.

"You shittin' me? Do you know we are on the sixth floor?"

"You got this, you're different. I see it in you."

Kayson hitched this breath and nodded. "I'll get her out."

Dex peeked out the door while switching off the light.

The men were close; three of them, and they had picked up speed. Only, the hall was filling up again with staff members and patients coming out of their rooms. Dex was thankful for the diversions.

. He exited the room, closing the door.

The sound of breaking glass vibrated from behind. His shoulders dropped. Dex ran at them. He smiled, hoping this would help his sister's getaway. Dex snatched the chains from his pants. He was ready.

"Get him!"

The guy in the front punched at him. Dex ducked and hit back then followed with a kick that slammed the guy into the wall. The guy bounced off the wall with a shake. Then punched and kneed him in the stomach. The guy was muscular, but Dex was a trained fighter. Dex blocked one, then punched upward, causing the attacker's uppercut to hit the guy in the chin. Dex wrapped the chains around the man's neck, pushing him forward into the blow of a tall, bearded guy.

Another, then another attacked him—punching him in the back before slamming something hard on the back of his head.

Dex shook himself to combat the dizziness and swung the chain at the guy's ankle. He tugged, and the attacker fell back with a bounce.

The floor shook, trembling as though it was a keg about to shoot off.

"What the hell was that?" one of the guys asked the other.

Dex kicked back, pounding the guy in the stomach, then did a roundhouse kick at the other.

"Knock him out!"

"How the hell is he so strong? He's not one of us!"

But I am a Vigilant.

"Don't know. Just down him!" the bearded attacker demanded.

As Dex twisted around at the voice, the sting of a dart pierced his neck. His muscles relaxed, and his eyes drooped just as his world shook from the boom of an explosion.

· 2 ·

Dex smelled rotten earth. He was sick of playing possum, but it seemed to work in most cases. Dex laid there and listened for any movement. Slowly, he opened his eyes. What was the point of getting up? He'd lost them all. His family, taken. EmVee...he hoped she'd escaped but doubted it considering that explosion. So much had happened. Too much death had brought him to this place. His friends from his school were likely enjoying summer vacation somewhere, ignorant of the fact that their home wasn't in Newport, Rhode Island.

It took a moment to adjust to the dim light of what appeared to be a cave formed cell. The opening faced an outer rock wall with no windows or another holding cell. Stalactites covered in moss and various shaped globes clung to the ceiling. The damp smell of it was sour. In spots, cracks in the walls were filled in by mud with spews of stringy green slime.

Dex didn't like jail cells. He couldn't escape them. First, the brief stay in a holding cell in New York, then one when he first arrived in what he thought was Newport, Rhode Island. Well, his mind opened after he made the biggest mistake of his life. He wasn't in Rhode Island; he was in a place called the Void. Some in-between place to hold magical beings and the humans that were kidnapped. Loving London was how he discovered that fact. London was dead, thanks to Jake's jealous streak when she tried to leave him for Dex. Taking the Soul Thief ring from the severed finger of his murdered friend and putting it on was just the beginning of his nightmare in reality. He thought making the prayer pledge that removed the ring and freed his captive soul would make his life normal again. Dex was wrong. He was far from normal.

His family paid for his screw-ups. Mistakes he never thought he was making. All he'd wanted was to play pro-football. He tucked his arms behind his head and blinked back tears that leaked from his eyes. Dex's chest constricted. His family was all he had in this hell. He'd failed them. The only place he had to run was home or the gym his father owned, but those were likely not safe for him. Maybe the detective could help him... Keith Whalen, Kayson's father, who'd arrested him for speeding past a stop sign. The detective had spoken to his father about the curious disappearances of the kids in the Void. Even though Whalen had locked Dex up to get his father to agree to use him as bait for the elite team of football players who were also Soul Thieves in training, the guy's purpose seemed to be in the right place.

Dex sat up at the resonance of footsteps, someone was coming. They were light with a hop to them. He scrambled back into the corner where it wasn't as well lit. His shirt had sleeves with a loose hood, and he was grateful for them. He flicked the hood up over his face, bent his jeaned-covered legs, and waited.

The dark figure of a male came into view just outside the bars to his jail-cave. "He's still out cold! I got this, gonna put the food inside."

"Make sure he's not awake. Benjamin said he was stronger than any human they'd brought in. Better be safe."

"Psst! Benjamin is the scrawny one of the team. Any guy

with adrenaline could knock him out. I heard this kid was trained in several martial arts by his parents who were pro-fighters – the both of them. It's skill Benjamin doesn't have." The guy laughed.

Dex squinted his eyes; the voice sounded familiar.

The other guy chuckled with him. "You're right on that score. You got this?"

"Yeah, remember, I won all my rounds in becoming a Soul Thief and kicked two of the varsity players asses during initiation. I could handle a kid cut from the JV team who couldn't get it together to compete for varsity if he tried."

What the hell? Is that Trey talking ish? Trey had gone to the dark side and joined the Soul Thieves earlier in the school year. There was no way Dex could trust him now that he was a Vigilant—a deserter from the Soul Thieves and elite football players on the high school team. Dex didn't know the initiation process into the Soul Thieves. They were recruited from the rising JV players. He bailed on it once he'd mistakenly put his dead friend's ring on his finger and realized becoming elite on the football team meant selling his soul to an evil shape-shifter with stone magic. Thank God for being human and having a free pass for stupid ideas.

Dex watched Trey intently, trying to decipher if the guy was his friend still, or foe. In a flash of movement, Trey danced his fingers in a rhythm of sign language they learned in training for the football team that said 'stay quiet.'

Interesting. Maybe Trey was a reluctant enemy still having some empathy for a friend who once saved his life.

Biting his bottom lip, Dex swallowed and fought the urge to move. His finger itched as Trey lifted his right hand and pressed the glowing orb of his Soul Thief's ring to the lock at the bars.

Another quick succession of sign language warnings from Trey: 'Don't move. He hasn't left the hall yet.'

"You need help holding the food?" Heavy steps started toward them.

"Nah, got it. See you on the upper level. I heard it's a full house up there."

The footfalls halted. "Right. Damn, Benjamin is with them. I better go."

"I gotta get in and out of the cell before the poison wears off. I'll be up there as soon as I get relieved by Brian."

"Good then."

Dex's muscles were rigid. The breath Trey released before he opened the iron door moved the dust in the air. Trey quickly closed the possibility of escape back in place. The lock clicked automatically. Trey's shoulders slumped, and he hurried to the middle of the cell. He crouched to put the wooden cup, bowl of rice, and some meat on the floor.

"I know you want out of here. You looked ready to tackle me when I opened the door."

Dex didn't answer; he just sized up Trey's stance. He knew from experience the ring that could unlock the door wouldn't come off unless Trey was dead.

"Why are you helping me?" Dex's voice came out hoarse.

Trey slid a canteen off his shoulder and poured water into the wooden cup next to the bowl. "I know it's been a while since we talked. Lots has happened since Grady's murder. London was found dead. I know you loved her, but she was in some deep shit."

Dex slanted his eyes. He dipped his gaze to Trey's ring. "Aren't you in it too?"

Trey's smile was sanguine. "Right, that."

"Are you helping me?" Dex's mouth watered at the food and water Trey waved toward him.

"I said I would. You saved my life. A life for a life." Trey nodded at the food. "Go on, eat. It's not poisoned. We eat the same time the human prisoners eat when we are on watch."

Dex frowned. Hecrawled toward the food. Anyone who didn't know jujitsu would've thought the movement a show of weakness, but Dex wanted to be ready for any attack Trey may attempt. Besides, staying low saved him from falling to the ground.

Dex stuffed the food into his mouth with his fingers, his gaze plastered on Trey's face.

"I'm going to make this quick. There is no way you can escape this place. We are several levels below ground, in a city not known to the people that live here in the Void."

His fingers stilled. Damn. If there was no escape, what was Trey getting at?

"There's one opportunity though: when you are being moved. It's the only chance you will have to get away."

Dex swallowed the last of his food and gulped down the water, narrowing his eyes at Trey.

"It will be a while before that happens. They don't move prisoners until the ward is full. You're the only one here so far. I also guard upstairs. It took about a month or two to fill up that one."

"A month? You expect me to rot in here a month? You call this helping me?" Dex tossed down the cup. The place gave him the creeps. Staying here a month alone would drive him insane. Dex knew it. Every documentary he'd watched on the internet about human biology mentioned that people go insane in solitary.

"Or sooner. We've had a surge in activity. Vampires, werewolves...even the faerie have grown bolder. They aren't supposed to interfere in the lives of the human families that are here or be here without permission. They are sneaking in and we haven't been able to track down how. The Soul Thieves are going after other rare species."

"Why?"

Trey shrugged. "They were requested by the head scientist, Sylvia. That woman is as crazy as the mad hatter ever was."

"Wait. Scientist?"

"Yeah, she requests the rare finds, demi-gods which are impossible to find, but some have been lured here and...the human defectors, like you."

"My family? Did she request my family be kidnapped?"

Trey stilled and held up a finger to his lip to get Dex to stop talking.

Dex dropped the bowl. He moved quietly toward the darkened corner, pulled his hood down just over his eyes, and leaned back into a squat.

Trey snatched the discarded dishes and kicked his canteen over to Dex.

"Trey? You here?" called a guy with a deep voice.

Dex crossed his arms over his knees as Trey rushed out of the cell and closed the door.

"Just feeding the inmate, he was waking up. I put him in a chokehold to get him dazed so I could feed him."

"Good. They need you upstairs. I've got watch down here."

"Thanks, Brian, should be easy. He's the only one down here."

The guy chuckled. "I don't give a damn. He's going nowhere. I'm taking a nap. They have us chasing some escaped bastard that is both Pied Piper and Rumpelstiltskin. Why the hell would they mix something like that?"

Trey laughed. "Scientists like to push the limits." His steps retreated.

"That woman is more than pushing limits. she's going to get us all killed by creating creatures that can't be controlled." Brian grunted and sat down in front of Dex's cell. "I'm not going after him. He's deadly, even eats souls. Hell, mine's already been taken." Brian chuckled.

Dex frowned. He didn't understand what they were talking about. At least Brian planned to leave him alone. He'd be damned if he'd wait as Trey advised. First chance he got, he would break out of there. Seemed like the best chance would be before more guards and prisoners arrived.

With a smirk, he observed every move Brian made. Maybe tonight would be the best night.

Dex watched his new guard from the corner, not making a sound as the guy munched on a candy bar, drank a soda, and farted while belching like he was in a contest with someone. Brian didn't look to be much older than a high school senior, but he carried himself a bit like an old man.

Tucking the canteen and its strap under his arm, Dex crept toward the bars of the cell. His guard was facing the opposite cell, leaning on the bars of Dex's for back support. Brian didn't notice Dex's movement since he was singing some rap song off-key.

Brian's two-way radio beeped. Dex stopped his pursuit and remained completely still.

"Brian here."

"It's Trey. You gotta stay there longer. Something called the Shadow Hound escaped, and I have to play water-boy to the Senior Soul Thieves going into the Wicked Darkwood forest to get him."

"Lucky bastard. Why didn't they want me?"

"You weren't here. Coach Moreau pointed at the nearest kid, and that was me, to play truck babysitter."

Brian laughed. "I'll be here. The soon to be test-subject is still sleeping."

"Out."

"Out." Brian snorted and tossed the radio on the floor.

Dex waited until the guy's shoulders dropped then

pounced forward, snaking his arm through the bars and around the guard's neck.

"Sleep!" Dex tightened his hold.

Brian jerked Dex's arm down. Brian sprang upward, breaking Dex's hold.

"You think you can sneak up on me?" Brian used his ring to open the door. He lunged in at Dex with a punch.

Dex ducked and kicked upward. The guard flew backward and hit the bars. He bounced off, and recovered, landing an elbow to Dex's jaw.

"Damn!" Dex shook his head. The guard was strong, super-human strong. Dex smiled. So was he.

Swinging the canteen by the strap, Dex whacked it across the guard's face.

Brian stumbled back. "You're not getting out of here." He spat blood, red with a bluish tinge to it.

"The hell I'm not." Dex kicked the guard's stomach. He elbowed downward on the back of the kid's neck. "Ah!" He bent his knee and collided his heel with the side of Brian's chin.

The guard fell back at an odd angle. Squinting, Dex narrowed his gaze at Brian's twitching body. He wiped the blood from his mouth. Damn. It too was tinged with blue. Dex hurried to Brian. He dragged him to the bars, releasing a grunt as he wrestled the limp hand up to the lock to touch Brian's ring to it.

The door clicked. Dex expelled the air from his expanded cheek. The guard twitched. Dex shoved Brian's shoulder down to the hard ground. He grabbed the canteen. Shutting the door, Dex quickly wrapped the shoulder strap around the lock. He tied it with the canteen hanging in front.

Dex waited with his arms crossed. Brian shook his head.

Brian hopped up. "How'd you beat me! I'll kill you." The guard struggled to unravel the canteen ties from around the lock.

Dex smiled. He touched his finger to his forehead. "Skill your butt can't fight." He pivoted and ran down the carved rock corridor. He tried to ignore the gag reflex from the sour smell of rotting flesh.

The corridor was lit with candelabra, which he didn't know whether they were lit by fire or electric. Dex didn't care; he had to get out of there. Every cell was empty, and there were many of them carved out of the rock that he guessed was buried within the earth. The only sound was cursing from the guard. The guy's banging was a timer in Dex's head for how long he had to find a way off the floor.

Finally, the hall ended, but it was another gated door of bars. Dex's head dropped when he realized only the Soul Thieves' ring could open it.

Brian's cursing stopped. His cell door banged open, echoing down the long hallway. The pounding of angry feet sounded behind him. Dex pivoted and ducked the moment a punch landed at the back of his head.

The guard's arm flexed, preparing to strike another blow. Dex smiled. He grabbed Brian's wrist then twisted him around, landing an elbow to his stomach. Dex wrapped the other arm around the guard's neck, forcing his weight down to make it hard for Brian to struggle.

"I need your ring." Dex twisted the guard's wrist and inched it closer to the lock.

Brian cursed. Dex jerked Brian's fisted hand closer to the lock.

Voices and the rumble of feet pounded toward them.

Brian laughed. "You're good as dead."

Several guards reached the gate. Dex pushed back, slamming Brian into the nearby wall. Brian recovered and grasped Dex around the neck. Dex surged his fisted arms up, but Brian twisted away, yanking Dex by the hair.

"Knock him out!" Brian yelled, wrapping his arm around Dex's neck.

It was hard for Dex to breathe, but he stilled and stared at the blue eyes of Jake, who smiled at him before sinking a knife into his side.

Dex grunted against the pain. Two of the guards yanked his arms, steadying him as they stood holding him upward.

"Remember me?" Jake sneered and landed a stunner punch.

Dex's last thought was... *I'll make him pay.*

· 5 ·

Darkness became his friend. Dex winced against the pain in his side. It was healing. He didn't remember what kind of blade Jake had used on him. Dex just knew it hurt worse than anything he'd felt in a while.

Dex sighed. He sucked at escaping. He'd never forget the video he'd watched of Jake choking London to near-death and the vampires that ripped her apart in the woods. Jake had left her to die after she refused to stay with him.

"Ugh!" Dex fisted his hands to his eyelids and struggled to sit up. The wound throbbed. He'd loved London. He bent his knees, forcing the sob down his throat at the pain that sliced his heart. Damn, he regretted the night Jake tried to make her silence him and she'd let him go instead. He should've known something was wrong then.

Someone cleared his throat. "Are you finished?"

Dex blinked. His vision was blurry; he felt drugged. Shaking his head, he focused on the figure standing outside his cell. "Trey?"

"Shhh...don't ever say my name. I'm not supposed to be your friend. Remember." Trey squatted and tossed two rocks into the cell.

Dex grabbed them. "What's this?" They had holes in them and appeared sponge-like and grey.

"Medicine, to fight the poison they've been giving you to keep you sedated."

Dex rubbed his forehead. "About yesterday..."

"You mean last month? Suck on the rocks. There's an antidote inside. They also work as a vitamin boost."

"Wait? Month? I..."

"Don't remember? The stab wound; it was from the scepter rock belonging to the master of this place. Only his prized up-and-coming elite get weapons made of it. Jake used it on you; it's why you aren't healing so fast."

"Why'd he use it on me?"

Trey shrugged. "It's his favorite. If you were human, you could heal from it. If you were a magical, it would seriously screw you up. Which are you, Dex?"

Dex nodded. "We all are human, right?" He lifted an eyebrow.

"I don't know what I am anymore. I'd say...I'm the damned. A Soul Thief in training to seduce females to transform into Soul Trainers. All to lead armies against out-of-control magicals in our universe."

"I don't know what you're talking about, Trey. We're in Newport, Rhode Island. My dad moved us here. He wanted to leave, and the last thing I remember is we were run off the road." Dex eyed Trey for any sign of betrayal or answers.

"You're not stupid. You remember saving my life during the pre-initiation to the elite football team. We fought off giant spiders to be worthy of wearing this damn ring. You saw a beast shifter that was over twelve feet tall transform into a man." Trey fisted a hand and raised his ringed fist to the bars. "All for this."

"Your brother? I know you did this for him, right? Did you find him?" Dex swallowed. He lifted one of the grey rocks to his mouth to test the taste. It was sweet and gave him a jolt like his first energy drink. He sucked harder.

"He's dead. The messed-up part of it is he was in my

initiation. I had to watch them kill him. The master, Cyrillus, wanted me to work for him all the time. They kidnapped my brother and held him until I made it over the first initiation. I couldn't even be happy to see him alive. My brother had been some sick pawn to convince me to work hard enough on the football team to make it to elite."

"Damn." Dex finished with the rock and put both of them in his jean pocket. "I'm sorry I didn't trust you earlier. I should've listened." Dex got up, actually feeling the stinging tickle of his wound's healing speeding up. "What now?"

"You wait. We have a big hunt going on in a few weeks. This place will be filled. One creature escaped. He can kill us even though we absorbed the master's magic that changes us."

Dex frowned. "Cyrillus. He's the man who was at the meeting with Grady, my mentor? Grady..."

Trey nodded. "Sorry about him and his sister London. They never found the killers."

Dex fisted his hands at his sides, and his lips thinned. He knew who London's killer was. He wouldn't say since Jake and Trey were working for the same team. "What is this place, Trey? Do I have a chance of finding my family...of leaving here?"

Trey gave him a sanguine smile. "Never give up. Make your own chances, right? Isn't that what you told me every time you beat me out for starting running back position?"

"Yeah." Dex sighed. "Is this place part of the police department?" Dex stepped closer to the bars.

"No, the police department is for show. The real crime and police force here is us: the Soul Thieves and Trainers. If we weren't here, everyone that was human would probably be eaten and tortured."

Dex frowned. "Why are we all here together? I want to go back to New York."

Trey laughed. "New York?" He snorted. "You're not even on Earth; you were stolen from Earth, like the rest of us who started as human." Trey flicked his gaze down at Dex's hand. "Man, you're in the Void." Trey looked back up. "I'm not human anymore."

"It looks like Earth to me." Dex acted relaxed. He knew something was different about this town. London had shown him that, but he'd just thought it was a fluke.

"It's not, and you won't ever get out of the Void. Know that with assurance. You don't have a ring, and it's the only key between the veils." Trey stepped back. "But when your chance comes to get out of this cell, take it."

Dex watched Trey's retreating form. He was royally screwed.

· 6 ·

The rock felt light in his hands. Dex drew another picture on the wall. This time of an angel, hoping it would protect him somehow. This place didn't have them, he was sure. In the year he'd lived in the city, he didn't remember even seeing a church. Nonetheless, drawing one made him feel safer. Too bad the other pictures were of werewolves, vampires, and spiders with the upper bodies of females all in various forms of attack. He wanted the creatures he'd seen to be bound in some way. He didn't plan the canvas; the drawing just took over him. Maybe it would stop the nightmares he'd had where he'd fought them and got torn to pieces like London had.

He threw down the rock, leaving the picture of the angel unfinished. Dex fell back against the wall. Trey had been the only one to feed him. The last few days, he said nothing, just spoke in sign language to warn him to not try and escape until he got him some help. Whatever that meant, Dex didn't know. Who could help him now? Probably, Trey was just hopeful...or trying to keep him from getting killed. Apparently, they'd had one guard at the outer gate, and Trey was the guard who could push food through the bars.

The rock was almost gone. He wanted out of there. It wasn't happening fast enough for him. He'd thought for hours about where he would go. Detective Whalen—Kayson's father who'd locked him up for running a stop sign during curfew. He'd seemed like he was trying to do the

23

right thing when he made a deal with Dex's father to infiltrate the Soul Thieves elite to get answers about the murders that had taken place near the school. Now that Dex had an idea what killed the victims, he didn't know if Detective Whalen would believe him. A Fenrir werewolf demigod who was his son's best friend. Nope, no way the detective would believe him, but he had to try to convince him to seek the truth. Maybe it would lead to where his family had been taken.

"I can't stand this." Dex tossed the rock into the hole in the ground that was his toilet. At least the strange rock seemed to absorb the stuff, and the cell didn't smell like a toilet. That was what he had to look forward to – a cell that didn't smell like his waste.

His chest hurt. Dex regretted everything he'd put his family through. If he'd stayed out of trouble, and not been so obsessed with playing pro-football, they never would have had to leave in a hurry. He'd put on Grady's soul thief ring, and their lives went from bad to worse. His father's business partners turned against him, and his sister got attacked while on a date with Silas Bane, the leader of some rock-soul band, who he knew Grady had fought with and probably been killed by. Dex should've told his parents what happened then. He didn't. EmVee had been injured in the attack, and Silas had disappeared. Still, Dex never told his father what he'd suspected. How can you tell your father your sister was attacked by a huge-ass werewolf that breathed fire?

A noise came from down the hall. Loud, sharp demands followed by the cries of a new prisoner. Dex wanted to get up and see what the commotion was, but he didn't want to draw attention to himself. He went to the corner of his cell, bent his legs up, and leaned back, trying to disappear. No luck with that.

He counted the times cell doors opened and closed. There were many, and it seemed to go on for hours. Yelling, scuffling, and fighting. There was a growl here and there too. Some even tried to run. None of them got away though. The guards gave them a beat down. It must be the more experienced ones; they sounded mean. Dex counted the blows and deduced that there were at least twelve guards and maybe double that in prisoners.

A guard stopped at his cell and hit a black baton against the cell door. "You don't get any ideas about escape on my watch."

Dex studied the large thick kid who seemed to have just graduated from high school. He wasn't impressed. If he weren't in the cell, he could down the guy.

He taunted the guard. "Why? You scared I will think you are weak as the other guy that I locked in here?"

"Not scared. Just giving you a warning. It's a full house tonight. Enjoy having the place to yourself. By the end of the month, you will be getting roommates." The guy smiled. It was wicked, and his eyes oozed hate as though he had a personal vendetta against Dex.

"Good. I could use some company." Dex smirked and stood. He bucked forward at the guard, hoping to scare his cocky ass.

It didn't work. The guy stood stock-still and licked his lips like he wanted the chance to put his hands around Dex's neck.

"Brian's my best friend. He got punished for the stunt you pulled on him. You don't stand a chance of getting out of here, you know."

"I could've."

"You are four levels down, inside pure rock, with double gated cell doors in front of each entrance." The guard snorted. "Now at full guard, thanks to you showing us that our defenses were getting sloppy." He spit on the ground. "For a wannabe JV football player."

"Glad I could help." Dex wanted to irritate the guy. He was bored and liked having someone to talk to even if the guy was a prick-head.

"Funny. Don't get too comfortable. I'll be back at night watch to kick your ass myself. Brian deserves to be vindicated."

"Yeah, whatever, man. Just you try." Dex ran at the bars and hit them, grabbing the guard by the shirt.

The guard hit downward, breaking Dex's grasp, while sneering. "Remember my name. Ronan." He stabbed the baton into the opening in the bars. A surge of electrical power pulsed through Dex's chest, and he fell back, stumbling to the floor.

"Ha! You are not so smart now." The guy smacked his teeth. "I'll be back for you." He turned and left, whistling.

Dex didn't bother getting up. Something roared; it sounded like a big cat.

He swallowed. First time ever he felt safer in a cage than free.

· 7 ·

He'd gotten into a routine. Pushups first, followed by sit-ups, jumping jacks, squats—you name it, he did it until he was exhausted. Then, he'd nap, tune out the growls and snarls from his jail mates, and do it again.

It passed the time until Dex got to fight. Every night Ronan showed up at his cell, unlocked it with his ring, and charged Dex. It was exactly what Dex needed to blow off some steam. He made it a point to lose every time. Dex wanted to smack Ronan in the back of his huge ego. Not to mention the dummy enjoyed winning, and it was the only way Dex figured it would ensure the brute would come back. Sad, really, that he'd started looking forward to it.

Trey hadn't been there. Dex overheard Ronan a few days ago on his headpiece talking about a team that went to retrieve a dangerous suspect who escaped a lab. Dex wondered if Trey was with that team.

"Just in time", a deep voice jeered the inmates.

It was followed by some electrical shocks and howls from the various creatures in the cellblock. Dex smiled; it was him. Ronan. Only, it sounded like there were other guards with him.

Dex stood, rested his back to the wall, and waited in the best spot to get Ronan to come inside. He'd realized that Ronan enjoyed taking the first punch. Didn't matter, Dex was ready for it. No pain no gain.

"You waiting for me, wimp?" Ronan stood in front of the cell.

Dex let his eyes travel to a round sack, or cocoon, that Ronan dragged up close to the bars. It was thickly woven, similar to a spider web, but in the dim light reflected a gleam of bluish-green tinge on the egg-colored woven surface. The thing moved.

Dex stood straighter. "What's that?" He swallowed. His heart raced in his chest. Fighting Ronan was one thing, but he knew from the nights he'd spent hearing his fellow jail mates' noises that they weren't putting humans in these cells.

"Company for you." Ronan lifted the cocoon that was the size of a hunched over five-foot body. He used his opposite hand to push his ring into the lock then kicked the bars open with his foot. "Try not to wake it up." He tossed the thing in with Dex.

Reflex took over, and Dex caught it. He dropped it to the floor.

Dex jumped back; his head hit the wall. He slid to the opposite side of the cell. It moved again, and Dex jumped toward the cell entrance. "Get it out of here!"

Ronan struck him with the baton, giving Dex a shock that pushed him back.

Ronan snorted, pressing the baton deeply in Dex's chest, not allowing him forward. "Scared? You should be. But not of that. Of the other roommate you are getting."

Creaking wheels from a cart echoed through the hall. It was louder than the noise from the others. Dex's muscles tightened in his back as his eyes clashed with Trey's who was on the opposite side of the bars.

Ronan gave Dex a hard push. Dex stumbled back but, without hesitation, surged toward the entrance. Ronan punched at his face. Dex blocked it, and Ronan tasered him with the stick, forcing Dex back within the cell.

"Stop!" Trey demanded. "He's secure."

Dex stumbled into the cell until his back hit the wall. Something about Trey's words made him feel a bit safer. It was the tone, as though Trey wanted to say something else but couldn't.

Trey basically had this kid, about Dex's age, strapped to some type of hand cart. He was wearing a mask that reminded Dex of the thriller movie he watched with his mom named something like silence with some lambs. The silver-headed boy had green eyes and freckles on his exposed cheeks. A metal mask covered most of his face and seemed to have a mouthpiece jammed down the boy's throat. The boy's silver hair sprouted upward in a sweeping motion as though it was caught in a big wind.

Ronan stepped back as Trey wheeled the kid into the cell.

Dex wanted to bolt again, but he didn't. Trey's eyes warned him.

Ronan stood, legs wide, slapping his black stick in the palm of his hand. "I dare you to try it again."

Trey adjusted the handcart then secured it to a hook on the wall.

"What did he do?" Dex rubbed his fingers on his palm.

Trey smirked so that only Dex could see it. "Escaped, three times, from various locations."

Ronan snorted. "Apparently, he hates getting doped up on the dark magic that our head scientist is using on him."

Trey pointed at the boy. "He's a Siphoner and has a bad habit of using music to sedate his victims. Afterward, he darts them with some type of spike he spits out and comes back to drain their essence later when he's hungry—if they are lucky. But when he decides to kill on sight, he uses his fingers, sharp tongue, or music to suck the soul from his victims."

"Until he gets too full. That's when he's the weakest." Ronan chuckled. "Greedy bastard sucked three of the powerful Soul Thieves dry. So you have some time before he wants to eat you."

Dex wiped a hand down his face. "Why didn't you put him with one of those animals in the other cells?" Dex hoped he wasn't whining. He didn't want the guy in there with him. The boy stared at him as though sizing him up.

"The shifters, magicals, and vamps are too easily manipulated by him. Besides, they will be killed for violations of treaties or shipped to the lab anyway. You're the only human in here, so..." Trey shrugged, then used sign language to send Dex a secret message, *be his friend, and he will help you and her escape.*

Dex frowned. *Her?* Dex responded in sign language. He looked down at the thickly woven cocoon.

Trey left the cell, and Ronan closed the door behind him.

"He's too dangerous for us newbies to guard. One of the stronger Soul Thieves will be on lookout tonight." Trey put his hands on his hips. "Be good to him. He's a mean one."

It took every bit of will power he had in him to wait until they left and the last footstep faded. Dex hit his fist against the wall. "What the hell!" He wasn't just afraid of what was in the other cells. Now they put one of their most dangerous magicals in the cell with him. Be friends with him? Trey must be setting him up. No way those predatory green eyes, disguised in the face of another teenager, could be anyone's friend.

· 8 ·

Dex's skin crawled. At least it felt like it. Four days had passed since his cell was invaded by the staring-eyes kid and whatever it was in the cocoon that had fitful dreams. Dex counted down the days by timing the shifts of the guards. Trey had been the afternoon shift guard the last few days. The first day, he asked Trey the time in sign language. Trey chuckled and told him 'sometimes, it's better to not know.'

"Bull, I need to know the time so I can count how long I have to be in here before I bust out," Dex muttered then felt the tingle from the unflinching gaze of the boy. The guards never fed it. Trey told him the creature didn't require real food. Of course, if he'd consumed souls recently...

It was likely nighttime. The guard, Tom, was on watch, and he usually dozed. Each day, the other creatures in the adjoining cells were slowly being culled. The other day, the air was doused with the unusual, tormented animal cries. Trey told him they had to destroy the ones spreading the infection.

Dex did his pushups again, bored since Ronan hadn't returned due to some promotion he'd gotten. After his set, he did some shadowboxing to music he imagined in his head. He didn't know the melody, but it was haunting. Dex stopped and pivoted toward the boy. "Are you making the music?"

31

The boy's eyebrows raised.

Dex shook his head to clear the melody. "Don't do that. I'm not a bad guy. I don't like people playing with my mind."

The music stopped.

A deep gravelly sound like a suppressed cough came off the guy. Rubbing his fingers together, Dex peeped at the guard whose head was drooped to his chest.

"If I loosen the headpiece, do you promise to lay low so they don't come in here and kill us?"

The boy's eyes widened then relaxed.

"Blink two times for yes, and one time for no."

Dex waited. The creature's eyes didn't budge for what seemed like hours. Finally, the boy blinked twice.

Sweat formed on Dex's forehead. He looked down at the cocoon for some type of assurance that he was doing the right thing. The thing within it was still, for once, seeming to give no answer at all to whether loosening the headpiece was wise.

He rubbed his hands together. Slowly, he walked closer to the boy. The contraption on his head seemed like it was something they'd pieced together in order to contain him, and since it worked, they didn't improve upon it. Maybe they were afraid to risk it. The guards had started wearing earpieces. Maybe it was to protect them.

"Do you know how to open this thing?" Dex fiddled with the lock on the back.

The boy blinked twice.

"Can you tell me?"

The boy's eyebrows dipped in a frown.

"You need to put that song back in my head to tell me?" That thought didn't make Dex too comfortable. Since the experience he'd had when he put on the discarded Soul

Thief ring from his friend Grady's finger, he didn't like anything messing with his mind.

Dex counted the slow two blinks.

"Don't put nothing else in my head. I know you've been screwing with the guard. No way he would normally fall asleep every night." There was a flicker of amusement in the boy's eyes. "I'm ready." Dex closed his eyes and waited.

His head filled with a deep grumbling of a melody. Before long, he was lost in the baritone beats that sounded stilted here and there. There was a faint echo of a click and the melody stopped.

Dex blinked, shaken to realize his hands were holding the headgear which had been over the boy's face. The guy's face was only a few inches below Dex's. He had no recollection how he'd taken the thing off.

The boy smiled. "I'm Nash."

Dex shook his head, stumbled back, and dropped the metal headpiece. "Damn." Dex's rapid breathing stopped him from saying what he was thinking. Nash was a sneaky bastard. *Friends. Try to be his friend.* "I'm Dexter, but call me Dex." He glanced down at Nash's flexing hands. "You want me to loosen your wrists."

"You better not. Sometimes, I reach for things when I shouldn't."

"O-kay." Dex stepped back a bit.

Nash looked down at the cocoon on the floor. "She is healing. Something tried to kill her while she was hiding from the Soul Thieves in the woods."

Dex frowned. "How do you know?"

Nash attempted to shrug, but the contraption he was secured to only squeaked. "They picked her up on their way here with me. My music can't penetrate her protective cover."

"What is she?" Dex wondered if he'd have to deal with some type of hideous monster when she broke free.

"Half-breed. Pixie and human. The Soul Thieves were excited at finding her. They want her to be taken for testing by their scientist, who's a Soul Trainer witch."

"Soul Trainers are witches?" Dex's ex-girlfriend, London, was a Soul Trainer. She wasn't a witch. If she were, maybe she wouldn't have been murdered. Only women were the trainers, and the guys were the Soul Thieves that recruited and sponsored them. At least that's what he'd discovered by the time his family tried to escape.

"No, they aren't." Hate blossomed on the boy's appealing features. "Sybil is though. She stole alchemy secrets from scrolls of the fallen angels. Then lured one here for its power."

"Uh-huh." Dex nodded. His mind warred with what this boy-creature revealed about the place he'd thought was Newport, Rhode Island. Now, it was a prison for him and creatures he'd only seen in movies.

"Do you want to escape here? I can help you." Dex wanted out of this place.

Nash smiled. "Yes, but now is not the time. We have to wait for her to hatch. I need her for a successful escape. It's why I implanted a song in the guard's mind to put her with me."

"You manipulated my friend, Trey?" Dex wiped a hand down his face. This guy Nash was dangerous. Dex could feel it, only now, he felt it was time to stop being the nice guy. He would survive. Finding a way to save his family started with getting out of here even if making a deal with this little devil would do it.

Nash lifted an eyebrow. "I hummed him a tune."

"Whatever. You want my help getting out of here? I'm offering as long as we go our separate ways."

"I will take your willing help." Nash cocked his head to the side. "Although, if I wanted it, I could make you give it, you know."

Dex crossed his arms over his chest. "Isn't a free give better?"

"Oh, it is. What will you give me for helping you get free?"

Dex frowned. "Give you? I got nothing."

"Everyone has...something."

"What are you? I like to know what kind of creature I'm bargaining with." Dex didn't want to give this imp anything.

"I am many things, yet, in part, *not a* human like you."

Dex caught a hint of regret in his tone. He could swear Nash bore a hungry gleam in his eye. Trey had warned him that Nash was Pied Piper and Rumpelstiltskin. Dex knew the Pied Piper had something to do with music. He had no idea what a Rumpelstiltskin was, and he had a feeling he shouldn't mention it to Nash.

"You need to tell me specifically what you want before I can agree to anything."

One side of Nash's lips kicked up. "Her. The pixie-human. Give me her."

Dex frowned. He scratched his head. Why would Nash want something like that? The girl wasn't his to give. He didn't even know what it looked like. "Not mine to give."

Nash shrugged. "Well, I won't help either of you."

"Wait! Fine, sure, you can take her with you."

Nash smiled widely. "When it's time, I'll collect. I will get us out of here. Now, put the mask back on me. More guards are coming."

For some reason, Dex felt that he had made a mistake. Even though he didn't know the female creature in the cocoon, he wondered at Nash's request. Dex swallowed, and a lump formed in his chest.

He said, "I hope I don't regret this," but he already did.

T hey'd been killing the prisoners. The screams had changed from bestial to human—and remained unnatural in their tones. It usually happened during scuffles to subdue them before the slaughter.

Every night, he freed Nash so they could plot and plan. Sometimes, they just talked. Then he'd direct Dex to put his headgear back on just moments before the place filled with Soul Thieves there to pick off another jailed creature for the night. The guards played with their victims in the cruelest ways. He swore the growls had turned into human pleas for help before the sound of flesh slicing quieted them.

Dinnertime had come. Trey was at the door to their cell. Nash was locked up with his headpiece tightly in place. Dex stood relaxed against the wall.

"I brought extra food tonight." Trey pushed the food through the smaller opening at the foot of the bars. "He'll need some since I'm sure the feeding he had when he was captured has worn off. See if he will eat actual food and not people."

"If I give him this, he'll have to go to the bathroom. Is someone going to loosen his bindings?" Dex observed Trey to make sure Nash wasn't controlling him.

Trey eyed Nash for a moment. "You can do it. The guards are wearing earpieces that are supposed to block his melodies. Your chance will come when they kill the final two infected shape-shifters here in this cellblock. The

37

hunters are tracking more, and this place will fill up again soon."

Dex stepped forward. "Wait, what? Infected shape-shifters?"

"They are called sago, which means rabid shift. Instead of shifting from human form to animal form, they appear human but have the madness of their animal-self. They eat people, are inhumanly strong, and it takes many Soul Thieves to take them down. Not the prettiest things either. They stay in the woods since it calls to their animal form, but lately, they've been moving into the public areas."

Dex gulped. "Is that what most of the other cells are filled with?"

"Yeah, the disease is spreading. Our scientists are working on a cure, but until then, it is capture, bleed them for research, then kill them."

"What happened to Ronan?"

"He got promoted to hunter. He is a high school grad-uate now, so he has to act like it until his time comes around to repeat high school or do college. Whichever he decides."

"Repeat high school?" Dex's jaw dropped.

"We don't age fast and don't want humans who don't know about the underworld here in Rhode Island to start investigating. So, we disappear from that generation until we are given the clear to return to high school and do it all over again."

"O-kay..." Dex didn't want to ask more about it. He seri-ously wondered if he was going insane.

"With the promotion, Ronan gets to support the Soul Trainers who are luring these creatures into the open woods and catching them."

"I thought you got promoted."

"Naw. I have to work the cells and still go to football practice for summer conditioning until school starts back."

"Football?"

"Yep, got to keep the illusion going, right? The non-suspecting human inhabitants of the Void can't know that they have been trapped and held for the breeding of the next Soul Warrior from their family line."

"I was one of those people."

Trey gave him a sanguine smile. "Not anymore."

Dex wiped a hand down his face. "Did you see Kayson at practice?"

"He missed a few days. Out of the blue, he showed up. Why?"

"I was hoping to find his father. I think he can help me."

"I'll get the address and directions to his house," Trey whispered. "You will have your chance in a few weeks. Don't blow it. You're on the lab schedule for research. We'll be moving you and your roommates." Trey gave him a nod and pivoted away.

Crack.

Dex frowned and faced the cocoon. It seemed to dry up. The petite body within it moved frantically as if afraid.

He bent and peeled away the cracked pieces. A thick yolk colored membrane clung to the fragments. The membrane wasn't moist but seemed like rubber, similar to a hospital glove.

Dex put a hand on the female's head. He couldn't see her; she was in a fetal position with her back to him. The membrane moved in and outward as though it breathed. His heart raced. A pixie-human. Would she be evil like Nash? Fairies were the good ones, he'd thought. The pixies, Nash told him, were mischievous. Supposedly, they felt superior to humans, and because of their tiny size; it was rare for them to mix with his kind.

Her breathing slowed. Dex wondered if she'd worn herself out with the exertion of fighting to get out. He tried to break the membrane with his fingers, but it wouldn't pop. He bit his lip and decided to use the pin holding Nash's headgear in place.

Dex removed the pin at the back of Nash's headpiece. Nash just stared at him as if he was perturbed that Dex didn't take off the entire headgear. Dex raised an eyebrow at him.

"I don't want you manipulating her before we get her used to this place."

Nash released a muffled snort.

Dex squatted next to the quivering membrane and pinched a portion of it as he pierced it. The body inside didn't move. He held back a flinch at the screams from the other cells. The guards were working out their frustrations on one of the diseased creatures. It made Dex work harder at opening the membrane. It was going too slow. Frustration welled up in his chest, and a surge of adrenaline poured through him as he ripped the membrane in half with his hands.

The girl sat in the fetal position, her back to him. Her skin was toffee brown. Her long wavy hair was intermingled with brown, blue, and green strands.

Dex swallowed at the sight. The desire to touch the thick, shiny hair made him rub his fingers together instead. He didn't want to scare her more than their prison.

"Beautiful," he whispered. Her wings resembled those of a butterfly but were translucent with vibrant colors of green, aqua, and brown. They were wrapped around her front. The naked skin on her back smoothly formed into the wings wrapped around her torso like a gossamer blanket. Her cute, large, rounded bottom was covered in matching translucent hip-hugging mini-shorts that mysteriously covered her while appearing sheer.

Not wanting to upset her, he moved to face her while still on his knees. "Hello. Are you alright?" Her eyelashes were long and curved with blue tips. The eyebrows that framed her full eyelids were brown with a shimmer of blue.

Her eyes were still closed, tightly, as though she was afraid to open them. The girl's arms were crossed over her chest, but the same shimmering cover on her bottom half was in a heart shape around her full breasts.

"I won't hurt you."

A scream echoed through the cellblock. The girl shivered. Dex put a hand on her shoulder. She opened her eyes. They widened with shock; her mouth opened and let out a squeak as she jerked back.

"Dex? What are you doing here?" Her hand rose to her neck. She was shivering but pressed her hand to her mouth as though trying to cover up another yelp.

He had to be dreaming. There was no way that she'd be here with him. Dex hadn't seen the girl since the day he'd tried to escape the Void with his family. Jake had been her boyfriend and had stolen London from Dex before killing her. How the hell had she gotten here?

"Yori?" he croaked. His stomach dropped. *He'd promised her to Nash. Damn!*

·10·

She shrieked and pointed at Nash. "What? Who?"
Yori scooted away from Dex, her wings retracted into
her back.

Dex lifted his hands, palms out. "It's okay. Calm down.
Please be quiet. The guards will come."

"Why is he here? Like that?"

"It's to keep him safe. I mean, keep the guards safe. He's
escaped here a bunch of times."

Yori lifted a shaking hand to her forehead. "How did I
get here?" Tears sprinkled with silver slid down her cheeks.
"He...tried to kill me."

Dex frowned and cast an angry gaze at Nash, who lifted
his eyebrows as if to say it wasn't him.

"Who?" Dex studied Yori's worried face.

She lifted her knees as she pulled from his touch. "Jake."

"Wait. What?" Dex fingers clenched his fist. "I don't
understand. Tell me what happened."

Yori sniffled and rested her chin on her bent knee. "After
I gave you the sketchbook when school ended, I got a text
from Jake. It sounded urgent."

"You were still taking his calls after he stole my girlfriend and cheated on you with her?" Dex shook his head.
He couldn't believe Yori was so gullible. "I thought you were
smarter than that. At least it seemed like it when we last
spoke."

She bit her lip. "You see me? Now you know what I really

am. As a pixie-human, I would have been hunted if anyone knew my secret. I didn't have magic to save me. I'm not supposed to be here or even be alive. I haven't been able to use or call my pixie magic for as long as I can remember. I'd only ever understood how to be human."

"So you didn't know you were part magical?" Dex sighed. "I'm learning more about this place than I ever wanted to know."

"Yes and, well, no. I was told to keep it a secret, but it never manifested. So, I started to believe I was a normal girl. It doesn't matter anyway. Jake never really loved me. It was London he wanted." Yori rubbed her crossed arms with shaking hands.

Dex growled; he wanted to punish Jake for killing London and hurting Yori. "London didn't love him." Dex bolted up. He paced in front of her, stretching to rake his fingers through his curled hair.

"I think she did." Yori's hand covered her mouth. "Oh, Dex...I'm so sorry. This is my fault."

Dex put his fisted hands on his hips. "How is it your fault?"

Yori slowly stood then stumbled a bit, trying to get her equilibrium back. "I had the chance to leave him...and I couldn't do it. When he tried to kill me, I couldn't kill him. I didn't want to give in to the darkness of the pixie. If I'd tried to hurt him, I think the pixie magic would have taken over. If I released it, I may not come back...you know, I might not be sane again."

He wiped a hand down his face. "Forget about him. We need to concentrate on getting free." Dex didn't feel like forgetting about Jake. He wanted revenge, but revenge would have to wait. Getting free and saving his family was his first priority. He only hoped Jake would get what he deserved someday.

Yori wrapped her arms around her bare stomach. "Could you if he tried to kill you? Before he stabbed me, my pixie magic had been dormant. I believed I was more like my father—not...like her." She shivered at the mention of what Dex understood to be a reference to her mother. "Jake left me to die, and I felt the thickness of it bubble up and cocoon me in a protective shell while it healed me."

Dex frowned. "So, you didn't use any of your pixie magic before?"

Yori turned away from Dex, her gaze warily moving from Nash's head to his toes. "No, never. It's why I got trapped here with my father. They assumed...I was human and a descendant of the queen."

"Queen?"

Yori shrugged. "It doesn't matter. I am a descendant, just not one they can use."

"Well, getting out of here is something Nash promised me he could do."

Yori peeked at Nash again. "He doesn't appear to be friendly. He looks like he wants to eat me."

Dex's chest tightened. No way was he letting Nash have her now. He'd play along until they were free. "Don't worry about him. He's on our side."

Yori bit her bottom lip. "If you say so."

·11·

Dex left Yori alone with her thoughts and sat in the corner opposite of hers. Dex waited until she'd fallen into an exhausted sleep before he focused on a plan. Anything to turn back the promise he made to Nash.

He felt Nash's eyes on him, but Dex didn't respond by casting a curious glance on the sometimes charmingly evil creature. Dex rubbed his hand down his face, mustering up the steel he needed. He had to act like he wasn't disturbed with the fact he'd promised something to Nash just to get the creature's help. He wasn't thinking at the time he did it. He would have promised almost anything for freedom. Nash knew it too.

Why would Nash want Yori? Hell, Dex may as well ask. It wasn't in him to be deceptive, and he felt Nash would see right through him. Maybe it was best to just play things out and when he had the chance, ditch Nash and take Yori with him.

The apparatus holding Nash rocked. Dex turned. Raising an eyebrow, he asked, "You hungry for some meat pie?" Dex walked over to Nash and put the pie on the ground. He stood and released the headgear.

"It's about time...my friend. I thought you forgot about me." Nash's gaze bounced to Yori. "About her."

Dex didn't flinch but bent to get the meat pie off the

floor as he swallowed and faked calm. He stood and lifted the food to Nash's lips. "I went to school with her. She didn't look like that, though."

Nash's eyes glowed a bit. He opened his mouth. His tongue had a point at the tip, which he dipped into the pie. A faint slurping noise filled the cell. Nash consumed the inner contents of the pie.

Dex held still, stifling the desire to move away from Nash while the creature's mouth widened and his front teeth elongated into points. Nash took a bite, nearly scraping Dex's finger, and consumed the rest of the pie.

"What the hell?" Dex stepped back. "You did that on purpose."

Nash's tongue licked his lips and chin then slithered back into his mouth. "Sometimes I have to remind people what I am."

"Do you want the rest of my pie?" Dex wanted to change the subject. He knew what Nash was—a monster. One he hoped he could keep fooled until they escaped.

"Of course. Just toss it to me."

Dex threw it close to Nash's mouth. The tongue whipped out to grab it. Nash's mouth opened two times its size to consume it.

"De-licious."

"How did you get to this place?" Maybe if he could learn more about Nash, he could find a way to separate from him.

"I was born here—in the lab they keep trying to return me to. But, I won't go freely."

Dex crossed his arms and leaned against the wall. "You had no one? Did they torture you there?"

Nash turned his face away. "Love and torture can be intertwined. When they are...well, they created me."

"Did you love someone there?"

"I trusted and loved my creator like a mother. She didn't want me. Instead, she took another boy home to call her son."

"What? There were two like you?"

Nash snorted. "There is only one of each of us. He, a beast, and I a piper with mischief. We shared a lab-room when we were children. She named him Silas, and me, Nash."

"Silas? I know a guy with that name. He dated my sister. I think he's in a band where he's a singer and plays on the football team."

"He is probably one and the same. He went to school, had a mother, a family outside of the lab. Unlike me." Nash's eyes dulled to dark, then the brilliance of anger reflected within.

"You know, he went missing near the end of the school year."

"Missing? That's impossible. He was practically a demi-god. Unstoppable. She never saw it in him, but I did. His beast simmered deep within him. I guess, somehow, he kept it hidden from her. He is more of a danger than I ever could be."

"Is she the scientist they are taking you back to?"

"Yes, Sybil. She named him Silas after her. His last name was Bane, a play on a hidden affliction he had. I should have known she'd favored him over me. I was the oldest of her creations, made from a man she kidnapped at the edge of town."

"You knew your father?"

Nash turned back to Dex. "Father? No, his DNA was extracted. He's what you would call a trickster of sorts. I remembered seeing him with his red hair and piercing eyes, which stared me down with hate." A brief frown marred his face then returned to a false calm. "They banished him to the dark cells—graves for creatures they want to keep on ice for further inspection. He was made into a Sandman in case they wanted more from his body for other creations. After me though, they felt his DNA was too unpredictable. So there is no other like myself. The female DNA that was used was a Siren. Sybil was jealous of her and destroyed it. I remember the incident vaguely."

"You remember your mother being killed by this scientist, but you still wanted her to adopt you? That's sick, man."

"A siren never loves anyone but themselves. The seducer of men was never a mother to me. Sybil held me, kissed me, fed me when no one else would come near me. She was the first who brought forth my song."

"Maybe they fought over you?" A brief flicker of fear crossed Nash's face.

"No. It was because of him, the Overlord. Sybil loved him, I believe, but he...well, he was being seduced by the Siren and mentioned coming to release her the following day. The siren never survived to see the freedom she'd seduced him into requesting."

"Where would you go if you got free?"

"I like the Winter Woods. I can take her there with me." Nash stared at Yori with a flash of longing.

"To eat?" Dex bit back the bitterness in the question.

Nash smiled. "No. As a companion. Pixies are cousins to Pied Pipers; our magic complements each other. I thought I'd never find one here. Pixies aren't allowed here; they like to hurt humans. So a pixie-human is more than I could've imagined. We will suit." Dex swore he saw hope in Nash's eyes.

Dex swallowed down the simmering anger in his stomach. Not happening, Nash. No way he'd leave Yori with him. He didn't trust a word the deceptive creature said. Everything to him was food. Soul food. "Yeah, right. So getting us out of here... You have a plan?"

Nash smirked. "Always."

·12·

He was dreaming; there was music in his head. Dex felt the sun on his face, the sea air teasing his skin—and he knew something was wrong. His mind was in a fog, but the scene of the beach, the surf, it couldn't be real. He got up and raced down the sand. Dex tried to remember, had to remember, the last place he was.

Dungeon. Smell of rotten flesh and mildew. A guy, pale skin with green eyes that were jaded and predatory.

"Nash! Nash! Get me out of here!" Dex focused on the pieces of Nash's face he remembered. Slowly put them together. Something Nash told him about that not being his real name. He had to know or remember Nash's real name. What could it be? Backward, Nash seemed backward. "Let me out of here!

A blink of darkness burst through the beach scene. Dex pounded his hands on the hard rock floor. He opened his eyes, and he was back in his cell.

With a shake of his head, his vision cleared. A soft melody filled the air. Dex placed his hands on his ears and held in a growl at the sight. Yori took a few bites of her food and fed Nash a few.

"You're awake?" Yori smiled at him. Her wings had come out of her back once again and fluttered. The veins outlining the multi-colored wings glowed beautifully.

Dex didn't hear her; he read her lips, and he didn't return Yori's smile.

He hopped up and narrowed his gaze at Nash. "It's time to lock him back up." Dex hurried over to Nash and grabbed the headpiece off the ground.

"Shut up!" Dex pointed at Nash. "Do it, or I'll wake that useless guard."

Nash closed his mouth and hitched up his lip in a smirk.

Yori's lips pursed with a daze of confusion. Her wings disappeared in a flurry. Yori's brows dipped. She wrung her hands then wrapped her arms around her waist.

Dex slammed the headgear on Nash. "Don't ever let him out without me being awake. He's dangerous." He locked the gear in place. "His songs, they make people do things they wouldn't normally do."

"Okay, but he was hungry, and you fell asleep. Besides, I thought he was helping us get out of here." Yori crossed her arms over her bare stomach.

"He is, but he's tricky. Nash may help us, but he is only really loyal to himself."

Nash's eyes shot daggers at Dex.

Dex pointed at him. "Back off. I'll talk to you tonight."

Trey's yell came from the hallway, "What are you doing asleep?" to the guard in front of their cell.

A flood of relief filled Dex's chest, and he released the breath he'd been holding. Nash had put him to sleep while seducing Yori into feeling safe with him. Dex didn't like the sneaking suspicion he had that Nash was using them both. Though Nash's song didn't have Yori dazed like he'd seen the guards. Nash gave him a brief stare which indicated Dex was the only one of them he wanted out of the way.

If Nash really knew him, he wouldn't have put him in a dream state on a beach. Dex never liked the beach when they'd visited Coney Island or the Jersey Shore as a family.

He'd wanted to be running the alleys and the streets of New York, searching out a place to tag some artwork.

Dex waited for Trey to relieve the guard at their cell. He went to the bars while Yori stayed back against the wall, making herself seem smaller than she was.

"Trey," Dex whispered. "We need our chance." Dex tilted his head toward Nash. "Some people are getting hard to contain. He's putting the guards to sleep."

Trey studied Nash for a moment. "I was afraid that would happen." Trey nodded. "I'll make it happen. There is a way I can give you your chance tonight. They will transport you. You can release him, but wait until you are on the caravan. Horses pull the subjects in wood and metal boxes that have some type of enchantment spell on them. Yours won't, I will make sure to switch it with one that hasn't gone to the witch."

"So, we just have to break the lock to get out?" Dex used sign language to communicate to Trey; he didn't want Nash to know everything.

"If I have the stomach to do what I gotta do to make it happen. That means clearing out the other half of this cell block—by myself." Trey shuddered before he frowned. "You'll need a Soul Thief's ring to unlock it. If you don't..."

Dex raised a hand. "I got you."

Trey nodded and turned, standing straight in a guarding position.

Dex went over to Yori who was biting her bottom lip. Instinctively, he raised his hand to touch it, then put it down. Yori wasn't his and never could be. She'd been hurt too badly and, thanks to Jake, so had he. He'd learned from losing London. Falling for London was a mistake. She'd paid for it with her life.

He cleared his throat. "Look, tonight we will have a

chance to get free." Dex leaned in, getting close enough to whisper in her ear, "Whatever happens, don't leave with Nash."

Yori pressed back even closer to the jagged wall of the cell. "Why?" Her soft blue and brown intertwined hair teased his cheek.

Dex bent lower to get close enough to make his statement clear, but not for Nash to hear. Dex resisted the temptation to dig his hands into her hair to pull her close for a kiss. "He eats people after he seduces them."

Her breath caught. "Eats them?"

"Flesh and soul. Trust me on this, I won't let him do that to you."

She hesitantly nodded. "Okay." Her chin tilted up.

Dex closed his eyes as her soft sweet breath caressed his cheek. A faint but insistent creaking noise grew louder behind him. He stood away from Yori and turned.

His gaze clashed with Nash's. The creature rocked the apparatus, staring at him with a pull that was unshakable.

Dex could swear he heard the echo of Nash's song singing, *your promise*.

·13·

"We can trust Trey," Dex told Yori.

"I don't know. He was Jake's recruit. Are you sure you should trust him? Is there something or someone they want you to reveal to them? The Soul Warriors always have agendas." Yori bit her lip, her gaze shifting to the bars.

Dex frowned. There was a lot they'd want to know. He wasn't telling them that his father was a Vigilant, basically a traitor to the Soul Warriors, and that he'd become a Vigilant by accident. Playing dumb seemed to work in his favor.

"I got nothing to hide."

She stared at him a moment. "You're lying. Nash told me about you."

Dex's jaw clenched. "He's the liar. Have you ever heard of a trickster? A creature that bargains for things he wants when a person is most vulnerable? That's Nash." The hairs on his neck raised; he knew Nash was staring at him. "But he's on our side."

"I don't know. You were in class with me and seemed normal, but you wouldn't be here in this cell if you were human."

"Says who?" Dex shrugged. He needed Yori, and he wanted to help her. "I'm tougher than the average human. I trained for as long as I can remember as a fighter and a running back. My dream was to be a professional football player. I spent my life building up my super strength."

A blossom of a smile appeared on her face. Yori raised her hand. "Okay, I believe you *think* you are normal."

Nash started rocking again. The sound made Dex step back from Yori. Dex refused to let Nash's warning mess with his head. He was thinking over how he could get a Soul Thief's ring to open their moving transport prison.

"Be calm when they take us," Dex whispered to Yori whose wings had long disappeared. "Can you fly?"

She bit her lip. "I don't think so. I've never had them before now. I'm still..." Yori sighed. "...learning how to control the magic."

"You can't just think it and it happens?" Dex didn't know anything about pixies or magic. He didn't want to know about it, but he had no choice if he wanted to survive.

"No, I have to give up something each time I use magic. My body is at war with itself. An evil magic half is fighting my human side that's trying to be normal. It's complicated. The whole act is hard to explain." Yori sighed. "I'm scared to keep using it. My father warned me not to. He said it can change me."

Change her? Doesn't she realize that he'd changed, everyone that was dragged into this place called the Void had to change to survive? "Okay, but it would help us if you could fly." Dex paced the cell, doing his best to ignore the howls coming from the few creatures meeting their death by the guards—or maybe just Trey who was creating a reason to move them. There were only a few of the diseased shapeshifters left. He'd started counting them the night he arrived.

"They are coming." Yori backed up against the wall and fell to her knees.

"It's okay. We got you." Dex glanced at Nash who

nodded. He went over and loosened the headgear. "Remember your promise. You help both of us to get free."

Nash hummed deep within. *I will keep mine if you keep yours.*

Dex fought against gulping as he looked Nash in the eyes.

"Your hands? How will you break out?"

Nash's hum carried words through the song. *My song can move more than just bio-matter.* He narrowed his eyes at Dex.

Dex swallowed. "Just don't move until I say so." He didn't want to give Nash too much information, especially since he hoped to ditch the guy soon. He stared at his feet and clasped his hands together, willing himself to stay calm by taking several deep breaths.

The thunder of shots from multiple guns was followed by bellows and cries of the few creatures being dealt sharp commands. The silence was unnerving, then the murmur of a few male guards bounced off the rock-covered walls.

Yori seemed to try to melt into the far wall of the cell while Nash closed his eyes, feigning sleep.

Heavy steps echoed in the dark hall leading to their cell. Dex raised his gaze and clashed with Ronan, his former guard. The guy had changed; a scar slashed his face over the eye, which was gray yet seemed keen as though it still could see.

"Miss me kicking your ass?" His voice was deep, harsher than before.

Dex wanted to smile because now he knew exactly what Soul Thief's ring he would take.

"Nope."

Dex remained lucid as Ronan slammed him against the bars. It hurt, but he was used to minor pain from fighting and football. He wondered if playing into the pain would work in their favor. So he winced to see Ronan's response.

"Don't give me an excuse to cut you before we get you to the labs." Ronan's demand was loud.

Dex raised an eyebrow. Ronan liked inflicting pain and making sure his victim responded to it. The guy spoke louder to warn the others. Dex would keep that in mind for later.

Dex inhaled to calm his breathing. His fists clenched in the metal cuffs. He wrested while the other guard manhandled Yori, who tried to bite the man's hand that attempted to bind her wrist behind her back.

Ronan leaned in. "You like her?"

Dex swallowed. "Not even. She was delivered in a cocoon. I don't belong here with these creatures."

"I heard you do. You wouldn't be here if you weren't a magical. Humans are above ground, dumb to the ways of this void. Maybe they want to find out if you are really human like you claim."

Dex jerked, giving Ronan a bit of fight. "I don't belong here! My father owns a gym; my mother is a trainer. Why am I here?"

Ronan slammed Dex's face against the bars. "So what? He can't save you now."

"Why? Did he escape? I don't know what you mean. My father wouldn't have left without me." Dex's heart seized knowing it was likely his father did leave. He just didn't know with which sister.

Ronan snorted. "Take the rest of them and load them in the caravan cell."

Dex let Ronan move him out of the way while one guard tossed Yori's petite form over his shoulder. Two others carried Nash out of the cell by lifting him and the apparatus.

Nash seemed sedated, his eyes not giving away that he was still aware.

"Seriously, I don't belong here. Who can get me out? Who do I ask? I'm human like you. I played football on the same team. Please help me."

"Help you?" Ronan slammed Dex's head against the bars again then pummeled him with punch after punch to his back. "Your family is a pail of traitors—starting with your father. You will never find anyone here that will help you."

A kick landed to Dex's back. His legs gave way, and he fell on his knees to the floor.

"Now change into these before I drag you out of here naked." Ronan tossed some pants and a clean shirt with long sleeves on the floor beside Dex's head.

Dex gave up and lay limp. At that point, getting up to show that he wasn't as weak as a normal human wouldn't help them. It would only make him feel better—besides, Ronan would get his in the end. Ronan was going to be Nash's first victim.

·14·

Dex ached, but he remained still with his legs crossed and back against a beveled wall. They'd blindfolded him as they led them out of the dungeon or underground city where he'd been held. Dex didn't remember anything about the passage. Someone cut the elastic tie that held the blindfold in place. Maybe Nash, since the creature had the ability to escape and gifts that could lull even the most protected guard to sleep. It didn't fall completely; it hung in place, letting Dex peek from the top. He studied the wooden portable jail that was being pulled along by several horses.

He turned his gaze toward a light melody coming from Nash.

"Finally, you are awake."

"What? I wasn't..." Dang, maybe he did get knocked out. It was all a blur leaving that place.

"You and she were. They drugged you," Nash whispered. "She'll wake soon." His gaze traveled over Yori's slight form.

Dex's chest constricted. He frowned and forced the feeling of possessiveness away. "Why horses and carriage?"

Nash raised an eyebrow. "You were sedated, and they believe I was too, obviously. The creatures that live in this part of the forest, behind the mirage of the city you lived in, destroy anything modern. They act as though it's an attack on their magic. If you don't want to disappear or be attacked, you have to use what is part of the natural order of things here. Meaning, fit in."

"So how do we get out of this forest and back to civilization?" Dex balanced himself and pushed up against the wall, cutting his wrist with the handcuffs they'd put on him.

Nash shrugged. "You run and hope you don't get killed. If you stay with me, you will be fine. No creature here can hurt me more than the Soul Warriors can. They have a secret weapon that gets me every time." He sighed.

"What can I do to make sure they don't use it and we all get away?" Dex wanted Nash to be with them until they were safe. He'd deal with the threat of him taking Yori later.

"Just let me kill them. If I do, they won't catch us. Besides, it will feed my hunger and strengthen me." Nash's eyes narrowed. "For whatever attacks may come."

Dex forced himself not to react to Nash's undertone of a threat. "We have to take off their ring. It's the only thing that will unlock this cage."

"There are ways it can be done."

"Good, follow my lead."

"You want to be free of the binds on your wrist? Move closer and don't flinch. My control over my hunger is thin."

Dex did so hesitantly. He could break them with his strength, but he didn't want Nash to know the depth of the power he'd held at bay. He swallowed as Nash's tongue, seemingly normal and pink—compressed into a sharp point that had a small hole for slurping—slithered from his lips. The tip was pink, but the rest that snaked from the mask was black. Nash's eyes bore into his as a tune hummed darkly around them.

Dex prayed the wooden cell didn't jar. Nash's tongue seemed to have a mind of its own. It slid over Dex's shoulder, down to his wrist and wound around the chained connector to break the binds. When Dex was free, he went over to the far corner where Yori was curled up in a fetal position.

Her hair had fallen over her face. Dex took a finger to push it back. She was beautiful, but he swallowed, reminding himself that he and Yori only had dark lies between them. Her ex-boyfriend was a killer, and his dead girlfriend the victim. Dex willed desire away, knowing it was just loneliness and nothing else.

"Yori!" He shook her shoulder. "Get up."

She stirred. "Jake...don't..."

Dex gritted his teeth. "I'm not Jake," he grunted, giving her a final shake. "It's Dex."

Yori opened her eyes and scrambled back into the corner, wincing at the bite of the handcuffs on her wrists in front of her. "Where are we?"

Nash answered, "The Fated Woods."

She looked down at her bound wrists and tugged at them. "How did you get out of these?"

"I helped him," Nash replied. "Come close, and I can help you too." He hummed.

Yori gave Dex a questioning gaze. Dex responded with a slight nod while helping her to stand.

"Despite what he may have implied, I'd never hurt you, Yori." Nash's voice seemed to move through the small cell to push past Dex's ear and entice Yori closer.

Dex jerked away as if pushed. *How could someone's voice do that?* Almost act as if it was its own person.

Yori moved with grace. Her eyes were unblinking with each step toward Nash. Dex didn't try to stop her; he wanted Nash to free her. He wouldn't let Nash's hold over her linger though.

Dex ground his teeth and remained still. Yori turned her

back and lifted her wrists toward Nash. Dex blinked when Nash's hum rose through the cell; it was beautiful, haunting, and Yori leaned toward it. Purple and blue hues of vapor lifted off Yori and wrapped around Nash. She swayed under the seductive call. Nash's tongue languidly moved over her shoulder, down her back, to the ties on her hands. Nash broke the binds, and Yori turned with a seductive sway in her hips to face him.

Dex wanted to tell Nash to stop. Nash made a quick rise in the lulling hum, and that note felt like a choke around Dex's neck. The humming note Nash projected was a mist formed into a string that grasped the sparkling lace of magic vapor from Yori. It tugged Yori's magic behind Nash to release the binds. It bounced up and over his headpiece.

A creak and a groan came from the apparatus that held Nash. The apparatus stilled, then Nash broke from his binds. Nash chuckled while he ripped the headgear off. Dex watched in horror as Nash lifted Yori's wrists to his lips and kissed each of her hands. Yori's arms dropped. She stared at Nash in some type of love-drunk haze. Nash smirked, releasing a sharp note at Dex. Nash shifted Yori closer and kissed her. The bluish-green vapor flashed between their lips when Nash adjusted briefly to kiss her deeper.

Dex surged against the hold of the spell that seemed to choke him the more he pushed. He stopped and took several breaths. His eyes never left Nash's.

Nash ended the kiss, but his arm didn't release Yori. He nailed Dex with a hard stare. "She's mine. Remember that. If you try to take her from me, I will escape any cage they put me in to find her. I will consume every bit of you."

"What are you?"

"You will never know."

"She doesn't deserve to be a captive. I can't promise you can have her; she has to give herself away."

"No, she doesn't. You gave her to me. What is your word worth?"

"It's all I got." He never gave the promise to Nash willingly. He would keep his promise to Yori and make sure she was free—of both of them if necessary. "Let's get out of here."

Nash nodded and snapped his fingers, freeing Yori from his spell.

Yori shook her head as if coming out of a daze. "Thanks, Nash."

Dex fisted his hands at his sides and pivoted away from them to peek out of the one small barred window of the moving cell. Dex struggled to retain the strength that lay just beneath his surface. He had to play the weakling with all these magical creatures until he could get to a safe place. Yori was part human and Nash was bad for her. Dex was positive he was using her magic for some way to feed his sick hunger. He would make sure that they would escape, but Nash wouldn't.

This is not going to be easy.

·15·

Dex waited for Nash's signal. He nodded that he was ready.

"Yori's magic can break the enchantment on this cell," Nash whispered.

"How? She doesn't know how to use it yet." Dex shrugged.

"I'm standing right here, guys!" Yori poked both of them.

Dex winked at her.

"She doesn't have to know how to use it, I do. I absorbed enough of it to break the enchantment."

"You fed from me?" Yori squeaked.

"You were delicious." Nash smiled.

Yori shivered, and Dex swallowed down the desire to choke Nash.

"Will it open the door?" Dex hoped it would.

"No, we need a Soul Thief's ring for that." Nash raised a finger and inched close to the window. He started a silent whistle that seemed to ride on the howling wind in the forest. Dex felt the vibrations of the tone as though Nash was giving him a silent warning.

Nash's lazy smile confirmed his confidence in getting the ring. Dex swallowed, knowing the only way to get the ring off was by death, one way or another. He remembered his father telling him the best trick a fighter had up his sleeve was patience. Patience was a hard trick to execute. Looking at Nash gave him a sick feeling in his stomach like he was seeing a demon or some evil wrapped in beauty. If he didn't know what Nash was, he would feel safe. Nash showed him a bit of his true self to warn Dex that he was playing with fire. When given the chance, Nash would have no problem killing him and sucking his soul out for a meal.

"What now?" Dex took a deep breath and stepped closer to Nash to see out the window. Nash was tall, but Dex was too, just under an inch difference between them.

Nash held up a hand. "Let her magic do the work." He pursed his lips and blew. The shimmering blue haze wrapped the cell in its glow. Particles of it bounced on the horses pulling the wooden enclosure before enclosing the Soul Thieves riding the horses. It sank into their black form-fitting shirts that had silver leather armor on the shoulders, chest, and torso.

"Stop the horses!" The Soul Thief leading the group raised a fist and yelled, "Something's wrong."

Nash and Dex backed up. Nash went to the middle of the cell, just in front of Yori.

Dex cleared his throat. "Someone is coming to check the door."

Nash winked. "Taunt him. Tell him she is sick, get him to open the door."

Dex nodded then whispered, "Yori, act sick."

Yori bent over and started a loud moan and stumbled movement side to side.

"Help! She's sick. Get us out of here!" Dex shouted louder and louder. Nash pounded the door, then scratched it, checking to see its weakness.

Ronan's face appeared in front of the barred window. "What is she doing?" His dark brows dipped.

"Magic. It's spewing from her, making us sick." Dex coughed and covered his mouth.

"The other guy? Where is he? How is it affecting him?"

"It woke him up, he's..." Dex backed away like he was terrified. He yelled, faking a cry of pain.

Ronan shook the door. Cursing, he wrenched it opened.

Dex bent his shoulder low and charged. He widened his arms and hit Ronan with all he had. They flew through the air into a tree, Ronan twisting and yanking his hand through Dex's long curly hair to lay punch after punch into Dex's face. It hurt, but Dex tucked his face into Ronan's side while delivering a jab then kick into Ronan's face.

"Ahh!" Ronan yelled.

They landed on the hard ground. Leaves shot into the air and floated around them. Ronan flipped Dex onto his back. He lifted his hand, and a ball of white light formed into a metal ball. "I'm going to beat your face in. You are not messing this job up for me!"

Dex blocked the first blow then bucked his back to unsettled Ronan, who fell off and to the side of Dex. He grabbed the collar of Ronan's suit and yanked Ronan's head forward to butt it against his elbow.

"How are you so strong? You are human!" Ronan roared.

Dex stabbed his two fingers into Ronan's eyes.

Ronan kept punching and tightened his brace on Dex's torso, using his forearm to force Dex back down into the dirt.

A melody floated around them. Nash appeared behind Ronan; he smirked at Dex. His tongue lashed out, stabbing Ronan in the neck. Nash's eyes took on a dreamy gaze. His fingers grew into points. Nash jerked his victim closer. Ronan's eyes bulged. Ronan fisted part of the thick tongue shaped like a siphoning hose. Nash sucked his tongue into his mouth and reared back. His teeth elongated, and Nash took a chunk of flesh out of Ronan's shoulder. He chewed a few times before gulping it down.

Dex scrambled from under Ronan while Nash fed on him.

Dex stood and released a shaky breath. Trey crept behind Nash. Dex's jaw dropped. He snapped his mouth closed and took a step back.

Trey spoke some strange rhythmic language, which ended in, "...sleep Shanenashashe!" He pierced Nash with a syringe filled with a black substance.

Nash's eyes watered before closing, and his mouth went slack. Ronan slumped over, falling face-first into the leaf-caked mud. His skin grey. The glowing stone of Ronan's ring beat like a heart then stopped.

Dex whistled out the breath he'd been holding. Trey knew Nash's real name?

"That's how you weaken him?"

"Well, it helps when he is full of souls. It's easier to knock him out." Trey slid the headgear over Nash's face. Next, he effortlessly tossed the limp body over his shoulder. "You and Yori are free. Nash killed all of them but me." Trey winked at Dex. "I was supposed to cover the rear. I knew this would work."

Dex wiped a hand down his face. He never considered Trey being so ruthless, but then, he'd known the kid before his brother was killed in front of him. Trey definitely had a deep hate for the other Soul Thieves.

"Give me Ronan's ring. They have to be counted."

Dex bent and hesitated before removing the ring from the frozen finger of the dead Soul Thief. He never wanted to touch a ring like this again. It had been the beginning of the tragedy in his life.

"I can't." Dex kicked Ronan's hand away with his foot.

Yori ran over to Dex and stood behind him. "What are you going to do with Nash?" She bent down, took the ring off Ronan's finger, and handed it to Trey.

Trey chuckled. "That's what he told you his name was? Interesting. He must've trusted you. Usually, he gives no name. It's too dangerous for him to share clues like that."

"Well, what now?" Dex stepped toward Trey who was pivoting away from them.

"Run. Anywhere but back to your house, or to anyone who knew your father. I'll say Nash consumed you. He's the one they really wanted, and they don't know she was inside the cocoon."

"But Trey...what about you? Don't you want out of the Soul Thieves?" Dex raised his hand. "You can come with us. We could work together to get those we care about out of here."

Trey shook his head. "The Master killed my brother and my aunt. I'm not leaving until he is stopped for what he is doing. If I can't stop him, I am willing to die trying."

Dex frowned. "I don't understand."

"He has a plan to team up with the demons on the Earth Realm where you and I come from. He'll kill the Queen that is protecting it from creatures like this one." He leaned toward Nash. "It's complicated, but consider yourself lucky you didn't get recruited like the rest of us from your pre-initiation night." Trey didn't give Dex time to respond. He pivoted away and ran carrying the limp body of the creature Dex realized may have been a friend.

·16·

Dex cursed and threw his hand in the air. "I don't know how to get out of here."

"I do, but I only know the way back to the city." Yori folded her arms around her waist. "I know my way around there pretty good. There are places we can hide that no one will see us, and you can find out what happened to your family."

"Trey said not to go back there." Dex paced, kicking up the damp leaves in the pile in front of him.

"There's someone who can help us. He's a detective on the police force that helped my family get new identities."

"I don't know. There's no one I can trust with my secrets. If they realize I'm alive, I may not be able to find and save my family." Dex turned away from her to rake his hand through his thick, curly hair.

"My father's no longer alive. He was murdered. We don't have many choices."

Dex pivoted to face her. "Who did you say helped you?"

"Detective Whalen."

"I know him. Maybe he can help us both. At this point, I don't have any other choice." Dex rubbed his hands together. A chill built in the air, and fractured leaves blew around them.

"How do you know him?"

"He arrested me. Later, he let me go when my father made a plea bargain with him."

"Oh. What kind of bargain?"

Dex shrugged. "That I was to be bait for a killer that was murdering some of the football players and cheerleaders."

Her jaw dropped. "Did you help? I mean...since your girlfriend London was a cheerleader, and the rumor was she was also murdered by the serial killer."

Dex balled his fists. "I know who killed her. I don't think it was the same person who killed the others."

"Did you tell Whalen?"

Dex sighed. "I am going to. Lead the way back to town."

Yori waved at him. "It's going to take us a few days on foot, but I know a few places we can sleep and hide until we are to him."

"I'm right with you."

They'd walked in silence for a while. The forest was lush and green in some parts. Other areas looked like fall had started, and yellow-green leaves floated around them, carried by a wind with an unknown source. Yori made it a point to go around those portions of the woods.

"When we get to the dead patches, be silent. Dangerous creatures sleep in places that are unprotected by the wood nymphs. The safe places are beautiful in the woods, the dangerous places look like it."

"Got it. You thirsty?" Dex searched around for some source of water.

"Yes, I could have something to drink. There is a fresh-water stream ahead. We should make it before dark."

He frowned. "Nothing before then?"

"I'm afraid not."

"How did you learn the woods here?"

Yori bit her lip at the mention of her past. "My father was human. We lived on the Faerie Realm with my mother, who was a pixie. My father was a human who'd been captured as a baby. He was taken to the Fairy Realm by a trickster like Nash, a Rumpelstiltskin creature."

Dex fought against his initial skeptic groan at her story. He now knew what he believed to be a normal city in Rhode Island was a dimension that just mirrored it.

"So, your father was raised by fairies and pixies?"

Yori smiled, her shoulders relaxed. "You believe me?"

"Uh, yeah. After what I've witnessed since moving here. I am starting to believe most anything now."

"Well, they fell in love and had me. The Faerie Realm was under attack. They wanted to escape. So, they made a deal with one of the twelve. We were told the only place we could come was here since my father was human and my mother was pregnant."

"The twelve?"

"Yes, there are twelve realms here in Eversphere. They are ruled by magicals under the shape-shifter king that betrayed his queen for the ultimate power of the Soul Stone."

Dex snorted. "Is he the general over the Soul Warriors?"

"Yes. If you ever went to an initiation of a Soul Warrior, you may have seen him. Jake mentioned him attending the pruning ceremonies." Yori stopped and grasped his arm. "You met him?

"Maybe. How much further?" Dex would never forget his face. The man with the black eyes that turned into a beast in front of him had been worse than anything he'd seen in a dream, or in person, ever before.

Dex didn't talk, and neither did Yori. He knew she could sense his retreat into his thoughts. What had happened to bring him here? His father hadn't been honest with them. He'd always been the family screw-up. No matter how hard he tried to stay on the straight and narrow path, he never seemed to become the kid his father could respect. He was always trying to be perfect, and his father had secrets darker than anything Dex would've expected. His father had never told them he was a Soul Thief that turned into a Vigilant to destroy the Soul Warriors. Why he'd want to do that, Dex still didn't know. He couldn't understand why his father would bring them back here when they were safe living in New York and hiding from creatures that hated them.

"We are almost there." Yori smiled, her dimples making her face look impish.

Dex thought she was beautiful before, in a sanguine way. Now, he realized that he'd never seen her appear happy. How had he been so blind? He'd sat in the same class with her for nine months, studied her face to draw her likeness in some of the characters he doodled during class, but never truly saw her.

Now was the time to start. He needed her.

·17·

They made it to the stream at the base of a small waterfall. The surrounding area was plush with trees and grass. There weren't any birds, bugs, or flies in the area. Dex frowned and looked toward the sky. It was at a dull glow, signifying the approach of evening.

"Are you sure we can drink from here?" Dex eyed the waterfall suspiciously. He'd only seen one when his family went on a cruise trip to the Dominican Republic.

"You look skeptical. It's all fresh water." She giggled. "Trust me, it's good." She knelt. Yori dipped her hand in, cupped it and brought it to her lips to sip. Yori placed her hands under Dex's chin, and her eyes dipped to the water in her hands.

Dex lifted her hands to his and drank the rest. The water was cool and refreshing. It tasted like bottled water. "That's good."

"I told you so." She knelt and gathered more to drink.

Dex did the same. "Can we wash in it?"

"I wouldn't. This is the fresh water, but you can wash in the waterfall. There is another water source for that one, and it's best for washing."

"What about you? You can go first, and I'll look out." He studied her, gauging how she felt about washing with him nearby. It couldn't be helped. He didn't want her to get hurt after escaping.

"Okay, but we should be safe here. My father said this

place is protected. After we leave here"—she slightly shivered—"the dead spots are abundant forest on the way to the border of Newport."

Dex snorted. "Newport." He put a hand on her shoulder. Yori jumped, but he held it in place, hoping she'd get comfortable with his touch. "I'll protect us. We'll make it."

"Yes, we will." Yori stood. "Let me show you where we can sleep. My father left a marker there so I can find it. It's on the side of the waterfall."

Dex followed her through the plush grass, moist from the foam floating from the base of the waterfall. A small patch of yellow flowers grew at the base of a curved rock covered in moss. Yori placed her hand just under the cluster of flowers, and the rock lifted to reveal a small door.

"He said gnomes left it behind. My father had an addiction to collecting old and ancient maps. Unfortunately, he also liked to follow their paths. And it led to his death."

Dex stepped into the enclosure behind her. A rock bed with animal hides lay on the floor. Also, there was a place in the wall with ashes and a metal grate that seemed to be for cooking. The place had a damp smell to it. Small holes in the ceiling let in the light.

"This is not bad. I can sleep on the floor. You can have the bed."

Yori shrugged. "The bed is big enough for both of us. You don't have to sleep on the floor." She traced circles in the dust with her toe.

Dex didn't reply. He didn't want to seem too pushy about it. Truthfully, he was happy she was willing to let him sleep on the bed. At least it had the animal furs on it to make it softer than the dirt floor.

"I'll go wash first. Can you give the place a check over? Then you can go."

"Sure, I will pick some berries, apples, and herbs we can eat."

Dex followed Yori to the side of the falls. Yori jumped in the water, her shimmering cover-up over her breasts and hips appeared like a silver bikini with purple and blue swirls. It was similar to the texture of her wings. Her skin was smooth with the exception of a curved silver line on the side of her face near her eye. It wasn't there before Nash manipulated her magic. Dex hoped it wasn't a sign that something in her was shifting from human to bad pixie.

He turned away and followed the trees that surrounded the falls. Flowers were scattered at the base of some of the trees. Most of them were yellow. Dex leaned against the nearest tree. She splashed around. He was tempted to look, but he wouldn't. They'd been through so much he didn't want to mess up the chance to earn a friend. He needed one.

His father had convinced Dex and his other three siblings that moving here would be good for their family. He said he was finally able to open up the kind of fighting establishment he'd been hoping to have himself when he was a kid. Dex knew now it was all a front. His father was a Vigilant and made some deal with them to infiltrate the Soul Warriors at the risk of the lives of his family. Why would his father lie to them?

Trey said that his father escaped. That meant his mother was still here, and likely his younger twin brother and sister. Maybe Kayson, Detective Whalen's son, actually saved his sister EmVee by jumping out of the window.

"Your turn." Yori sounded breathless behind him.

Dex turned and couldn't help but smile at her hair curling around her head. It had been waved before, not as tightly curled.

"It feels like my hair hasn't been washed in months." Dex raked his fingers through his curly bush.

"I have a comb." She handed him a makeshift comb that was a jagged rock, but the pointed edges had been smoothed. "I made it."

"Thanks, I'll be only a minute." He looked down at the black denim pants and the grey shirt they'd given him. Dried blood stains traced angry tracks on them. "I'm going to try to wash this out."

"Blood is hard to get out." Yori went to touch a spot then dropped her hand. "I'll get some food. There's lots of it around here."

Dex nodded. He jogged to the waterfall. He couldn't help it, but with each step, he allowed himself to enjoy being free. A smile slipped across his face as he dove into the water.

"This tastes so damn good." Dex closed his eyes and took the last bite of the sweet meaty fruit. He tossed the small egg and caught it with his open mouth. The few candles they found lit the room with a warm glow that was accentuated by the scattering of glass-covered holes in the ceiling.

"I know. The eggs were a surprise. I checked where my father found some when we were here together." She took a small bite of her egg, and a smile bloomed on her face as she savored the taste.

Dex uncrossed his legs and stood. He walked over to the bed and watched the dying embers of the fire she'd used to cook the eggs. The thick pelts were comfortable. The room was cool now that night had slid in and the temperature dropped.

"I don't think anyone has been here since we were. My father left a lot of stuff behind as if he'd planned for us to come back." Yori sat on the opposite side of the bed. Frowning, she hugged herself and rubbed her arms.

Dex noticed her agitation and attempt at hiding her sadness. "Hey." He put his hand over hers. "I understand, and I'm sorry you lost him."

She shrugged. "Thanks for caring. This is...it's too much. My life has been a blur this school year. I thought it was going to be the best year ever, but it ended up a nightmare."

Dex grunted. "Don't I know it? I didn't expect this to be a

good year. I never wanted to leave New York, but I dealt with it. Got in some trouble when I moved here. The first day of school, Detective Whalen arrested me on my lunch hour for running a stop sign and speeding. That marked the disaster of the year for me."

"You left the school grounds during curfew? Bold." She elbowed him. "You were so mysterious to me."

"I didn't mean to be, but I just wanted to keep my screw-ups to myself. It didn't work. It's like everything I did to try to make things right went in the opposite direction."

"Well, I can see that. I'm sorry I was mean to you in Art class. I thought you were nice, but I thought I was in love with Jake. Stupid me."

"Don't say that. You weren't the only girl manipulated by him. London...her love for me got her killed."

"What? You can't blame yourself for London. She was like Jake, a Soul Warrior, and that means the dark magic in her would have consumed her like all the others."

"I knew what she was, and I didn't care. I tried to help her. She wanted it until Jake seduced her back to him."

"She could've never been with you unless she convinced you to turn." Yori shivered.

"Did Jake ask you to?" Dex wanted to know what happened with her and Jake, how he'd gotten her to fall in love with him.

Yori sighed. "He scouted me. I regret that he discovered my secret. I could never be one of them. My father warned me they were what he was running from. He had a map that was very important to them, and if he discovered the secrets to it, they would've killed him for it."

"What do you mean?"

"Never mind. I believe he gave it to someone anyway." She shook her head as if talking herself out of sharing more.

84

"You can tell me." Dex pushed himself up in the bed to slide next to her. "I'm good for it."

Yori studied him for a moment. "I said, never mind." She turned away from him and lay down.

Dex sighed and laid back down, turning in the opposite direction. After several moments, exhaustion taunted him to sleep, but not before he heard Yori's muffled cry.

·19·

Dex lay there, taking his time to get up, staring at the ceiling. Yori was washing at the falls. She told him she wanted to go alone. They'd been there for days. Dex admitted he needed the peace and the quiet of their refuge. Yori did too. Healing was a painful process, and he wanted to take time to get his grit together before going back to where this started.

They talked about a lot of things while there, really talked. He hadn't wanted to do that when they were in the cell with Nash. Even though Yori was sharing more of her past, she never brought up the topic of Jake. Her revelations about parents stopped with the details of how she got into that cell.

Dex didn't have a plan other than finding Detective Whalen and getting him to help locate his family. Yori just wanted to tag along. Maybe get revenge on Jake, which Dex felt was impossible. Jake had seemed pretty high up on the Soul Warriors' ladder. Dex just wanted to stay out of the guy's way. One thing life taught him: know when to fold in your losses and run.

"Dex?" Yori came in through the open entryway.

He hadn't bothered to close the door. Dex liked to have the fresh breeze flowing. It smelled so much better than their former prison cell. He never thought he'd get the scent of blood, waste, and sickness out of his nostrils.

"Still in bed." He sat up and pulled down his shirt.

"You want to go egg hunting?" She tied her hair into a curly bun on the top of her head.

"Sure, I'm up for it." Dex stretched into standing.

He tried to hold back, stay cool, and allow Yori to lead the way their friendship grew. It was hard, real hard because she was beautiful. Her vulnerability was obvious even though she tried to hide it, fight it. Something exuded from her that called to him to protect her. Dex didn't want to scare her back into her cocoon.

"C'mon, lazybones." She pivoted around, hopping on the balls of her feet.

Dex grabbed the makeshift basket she made out of leaves and branches. "You are good at this. Art with your hands."

"When I went on hikes with my father, I never wanted to leave. Creating things along the way slowed him down." Yori stopped and pointed at a tree at the far end of the waterfall. "That's where I found some on the first day. We haven't checked there, so maybe we can get lucky again."

"Where did you find them?" Dex shielded his sight with his hand against the glare of the sun.

"The first branch, but maybe there are some further up?" She stood with a hand on her hip.

"I'll get it." Dex set the basket on his shoulder and climbed the tree. It was pretty high up, but he kept going, stopping at each cluster of branches to see if there were any eggs. He finally found a nest with a half of dozen in it. He put the bluish-green eggs in the basket. Dex closed his eyes while he breathed in the fresh sweet air that he never thought he'd tire of before searching the scenery around him. From his high vantage point, he inhaled all the green and lush woods. He squinted, trying to gauge the distance to the darkened part of the woods that seemed ravaged by fire.

Dex's heart beat faster within his chest. Was he ready for what was waiting for them there? He didn't know, but once he'd licked his wounds, he would fight through whatever he had to get them to the other side.

Dex climbed down slowly, not wanting to break the eggs. Yori's eyes widened, and she smiled. "These are good ones."

They spent the rest of the day gathering herbs, flowers, and berries they could eat. Yori pointed out the plants and told him their names. She'd remembered everything her father taught her about the woods.

The modest home, resembling a moss-colored hut, was softly lit by the small fire Yori had lit in the fireplace. Only two of the candles were lit since they wanted to conserve them in case they needed to stay longer.

"He wanted me to memorize his maps." Yori bit her full bottom lip.

Dex approached her and gently touched her upper arm, holding still, hoping she wouldn't flinch away as she had on numerous other occasions. She relaxed.

"Did you?"

"I did. I drew them over and over again. My love of art started because of him. He knew I would create pictures from my dreams. He told me the dreams were so vivid because of my pixie blood. I think it was just the way an artist's brain works."

"I see vivid colors in my dreams too."

"The first map my father asked me to redraw was the one that led us here." She shivered. "I know what he was looking for. He just should have left things alone."

"What was he looking for?"

Yori removed the metal pot from the fire and placed it on the stone floor. She scooped out the eggs. Dex grabbed one of the wood carved bowls to hold the eggs.

"Revenge. I wished he hadn't. If he'd just left it alone, he'd be alive, and I'd be attending high school pretending it was real like the rest of the kids there."

While Dex listened, he spread the fur rug near the fire. He sat cross-legged and reached for the wooden bowl she handed him. It smelled fresh and tasty made from the herbs and eggs they'd found. He dipped the broth up to his lips and slurped down the greens and herbs with it.

"Hungry?" She laughed. Yori sat next to him and placed her bowl on her straight legs.

"You can lean against me if you want." Dex smiled at her, adjusting her body into a comfortable position for balancing her bowl while she ate.

She gave him a shy smile and leaned her back against his shoulder. "Tell me why you stopped playing football. I used to watch you run down the field. You were faster than Trey. You were gone for a while. When you came back, they benched you."

Dex winced at that. Yeah, he'd been benched. "Not a great moment of my high school football career."

"Maybe it was better you didn't stay in the spotlight. Jake recruited the stars for the varsity team elite. Once that happens, you're stuck." Yori bit into one of the eggs.

"I think you're right. I had a hard time when my friend Grady died. Later, when I came back to school, I found that London had disappeared. I was in a bad place then. It messed up my game, and being a running back, even going pro to the NFL didn't seem so important."

Yori sniffled. "You really loved her, hmm?"

Dex smiled at the brief memory of London that flashed in his mind. "Yeah, I did. She wouldn't let me love her the way I wanted though. She kept me at a distance." He shrugged. "She left me for Jake."

"I don't know if she had a choice. Jake had a hold on her, on me. That's the way he works. Charm you, manipulate you, and then take what he wants." Yori put down her bowl, bent her legs, and wrapped her arms around her legs.

"Hey, c'mere." Dex pulled her into a hug. "We are free from him."

"Are we? I just don't want to feel so helpless anymore." Her eyes closed, and tears rolled down her face.

"I could teach you to defend yourself. We can do it before we leave here."

Yori tucked her face at the base of Dex's neck. "I'd like that."

Dex fought the urge to kiss her and vowed he'd teach her to fight her fear as he continued to wrestle with his own.

·20·

"Yes, like that! You landed a good one. Keep using your kicks. They have better range than your arms." Dex dodged another kick to his shin.

"Gymnastics paid off." Yori twisted to place her hands on the ground and kick upward at Dex's face.

"I had to find a fighting style that worked with what you had." Dex dodged her kick and crouched to pull at her ankle.

She landed in the grass. "Uh! Cheap trick."

"Fighting is full of them, especially when it's life or death. Use the cheap tricks."

Yori sighed and sat up. "I can if I have to."

"Good." Dex helped Yori up with his hand. "You are a fast learner."

"I had to be. My father was smart and always in constant movement. I wanted to be like him until I met Jake."

"Are you ready to leave? You don't have to go to town with me. You can stay here and be safe." Dex touched the wayward bluish brown curl over her eye.

"I ...want to stay with you." Yori's eyes dipped down as she seemed to study something on her bare feet.

Dex placed his forefinger under her chin and lifted. Her eyes met his. "I want you to stay with me too," he whispered. He leaned down and kissed her full lips, gently, waiting until she responded. Yori's hands touched his stomach, trembling as she slid them up to his shoulders. Her lips pressed back against his as she stood on her tiptoes. Dex smiled into her lips. A gush of warmth spread in his chest as he teased her into allowing him to deepen the kiss. With a sigh, she gave in, and he held her closer.

Slowly, he released her and watched her put a shaking finger up to her lips. Yori stepped back from him.

"Yori." Dex's arms fell to his sides.

"What does this mean, Dex?" Yori covered her mouth with her hand. "We shouldn't. I am not ready for this." She started to walk off.

Dex grasped her arm. "Wait. It's okay. I'm not ready either. When is anyone ever ready? I'm your friend. Okay?"

She stared at him a moment before nodding.

"That's what you want most, right? I kissed you because I've always found you attractive. Since we first sat next to each other in class, I was drawn to you. You know that?" Dex fought the urge to touch her again. She was crossing her arms and rubbing them with her hands again. "I fell for you first. Then when you weren't interested...London helped me to move on."

"It wasn't a good time then, and it isn't one now. Dex, aren't we just feeling this way because we've been trapped together? And what about Nash? I kissed him even though in my mind I didn't want to. I am...I have to think and fight feeling this way. Weak and drawn in by guys that are on the edge."

Dex shrugged. "I'm on the edge?"

Yori lifted her eyebrow. "You always were. Arrested the first day of school, dating London, who happened to be a Soul Trainer, then friends with Trey and Grady, who happened to be Soul Thieves."

"I didn't know what they were. I made my own mistakes, but it's like trouble just finds me. I am always working toward making better decisions and acting on them. Just, damn, it seems that I walk into bad situations no matter what I try to do."

"If you are, tell me what happened to Grady the night I saw you both at the club?" Yori narrowed her gaze.

"What do you mean?" Dex swallowed. He never told anyone about him following Grady after his fight with Silas Bane. Silas was the manager and lead singer of the band Dark Knights.

"I saw you!" Yori was shaking. She stepped back. "I stayed until the police came. The next day there were whispers around the school that Grady was murdered. You were there. I saw you follow them." She crossed her arms in front of her.

"Did you tell anyone?" Dex's throat felt like it was on fire. If anyone knew he was with Grady, it could be why his father had to go on the run.

"What? Are you actually asking me if I told someone I thought you murdered Grady—London's brother?" Yori stepped back.

"It's not what you think. I didn't murder him." Dex took a step toward her.

"No." Yori pointed at him. "You stay there and tell me the truth."

"Why didn't you ask me this before? When we were in the cell?"

"Are you kidding? I was in the cell with you and a creature that wanted me for his own. I had more to worry about. Like how to stay calm and alive. I got to know you, and it just didn't add up. You didn't seem like Jake at all. But I couldn't shake seeing you there."

Dex sighed. He felt he should tell her. Yori had been honest with him. He couldn't blame her for being scared in a cell with two guys for as long as they had been stuck there together.

"I didn't get into the club until after Grady was already there. He and Silas, the manager of the band Dark Knights, had an argument because he wouldn't let Grady into the band."

Yori crossed her arms and frowned. "Of course, he wouldn't. He hated them. He was the mysterious type. He couldn't be recruited into the Soul Warriors. The coach acted scared of him; Jake told me. He and Jake never got along."

"He turned into a beast, like a werewolf or something. Only, he had fire coming out of his mouth and eyes." Dex released air he'd been holding in his chest while gauging her reaction. She bit her bottom lip.

"You are saying that Silas Bane, first-string quarterback of the varsity football team last year and Jake's arch-rival was a werewolf?" Yori laughed. "Jake and the other Soul Thieves on the team would have known it and tried to kill him."

"More than a werewolf, like, a huge, fire-breathing thing that could be a werewolf but super-sized." Dex lifted an eyebrow. "He went missing before the end of the school year, after London's death."

Yori nodded. "Yes, that's when Jake got promoted to full-time quarterback." She shook her head. "He wouldn't have been able to conceal that kill from me. I watched him closely. I had to know if he would be able to find out my secret."

"You don't know for sure. I don't know what happened to Silas, but I do know what he did to Grady. I tried to fight him off and got thrown into a tree and knocked out cold."

"So Silas killed Grady?"

"Yep." Dex raked his hand through his hair. "When I woke up, Grady was in pieces."

"You ran without telling the police or confronting Silas?"

"Uh, I tried confronting him there and got tossed into a tree while he devoured my friend."

"What happened to you after that night? No one saw you for almost three weeks."

Dex dragged his hand down his face. "I took Grady's ring to give it to London."

"His ring?" Yori bit her lip and frowned.

"He was a new Soul Thief. I didn't know what the ring meant. I thought it was for the elite players who got selected for the recruitment by a college that would lead to the pro ball ops for the NFL. That's what I was told anyway."

"All the college football players and NFL players here in the Void are Soul Thieves, Soul Trainers, and their protégé's. You don't get to play sports here unless the *twelve* can use you for other things. Like controlling the other realms of magicals."

"I didn't know that."

"If you took his ring, you know they would kill you for it?"

"I didn't know until I put it on." Dex sighed.

"You what?" Yori covered her mouth. "How could you survive? The rings are evil magic."

"It made me sick. Someone helped my father take it off of me. It had to do with the gift of being human, specifically tied to what you are calling the Earth Realm."

"You returned to school like nothing happened." She whistled.

"I had to. My family...they were in danger because of me taking that ring. London died by Jake's hand because she loved me. Yori, I'm asking you to trust that I am here for you.

I need a friend right now, just like you. I told you my deepest darkest secrets. Can we start over?"

"Thank you for doing that, but..." She put her palm on his chest and stepped back. "I need some time alone to think about this...don't follow me." Yori pushed past him, jerking away from Dex's outstretched hand.

He didn't blame her for her mistrust. He'd treated her like crap after he started dating London. Not telling her what happened before the kiss, that was a bad move on his part. Dex wanted her to come with him. It was selfish, but he needed the comfort of her calm spirit and her friendship.

Seemed like he'd just screwed himself out of the chance to claim it.

·21·

Dex was worried. Yori had been gone most of the day, and now it was night time. He'd promised he would give her time. Though, to be honest, he'd hoped she'd come back to their tiny home. Instead of waiting patiently, he'd followed her for a bit and realized she was going in the opposite direction of the home. She spotted him and yelled at him to leave her alone.

He did, going to the waterfall for a dip instead, then laid out in the sun with his clothes on to dry and think. Afterward, he picked some berries, herbs, and found some eggs, wrapping in his shirt, then headed back to the home, hoping she was there, which she wasn't.

"I've got to get her." He paced the small quarters. He did pushups, sit-ups, boxing warm-ups, and none of it calmed the anxiety he had at her being out of his sight for this long. He cooked and set the warm food on the table wrapped in a small piece of cloth.

He couldn't wait any longer. Pacing wasn't bringing her back. Dex left the home and headed in the direction he'd seen her going. There was enough of a glow from the moon-light to light his path. Even so, it didn't matter. The changes from putting on Grady's ring made him different. He had some of the abilities of the Soul Warriors but without the chains of the evil that bound them. It was a gift, the depths of which he was still getting to know, and he was told never to reveal it. He couldn't see in the dark, but he sensed things.

Too many lives were at stake if he was taken over by the dark powers of Grady's Soul Warrior ring. Being a Vigilant was something his father had done; it was also what likely made his father come to the Void after living freely in the Earth Realm for as long as Dex could remember. His dad had been concerned that he would die and become some type of pawn for Cyrillus. Sometimes he wondered if he was to have gone whether his family would've been safe. *Fight it, live, fight to live* is what his father chanted to him. Life was a better chance to get things right, but to give in to death was to end with the failure of never even trying.

He'd didn't go too far away from the falls before he saw her. Dex stopped, mesmerized by the beauty in front of him. On a rock with her knees up, arms around them and head down, Yori's hair glowed with blue highlights. Her wings were fully extended from her body, translucent with shivering veins of gold, green, and blue that throbbed in unison to her heartbeat. It was the first time since their cell she had her wings extended.

"Yori?" Dex slowly walked toward her.

She lifted her eyes to his, and the tears glowed blue. "I can't get them to go away." Her whisper was broken. "It's the evil in me coming out. I hate it."

Dex approached her slowly. "No, it's not. You aren't evil. Losing control of something powerful is expected. That's why when training young fighters, we caution them to be careful."

Her wings fluttered. "I thought I was careful. I haven't had to do this before. They never manifested until Jake hurt me."

Dex inhaled to calm his beating heart and think about what to say to her. "What happened, and when did you notice them?"

"I was so angry at you...myself, I ran here. I was stomping and hitting this rock. Before I knew what was happening...I was flying. Just a little above the rock. When I realized what I was doing, I fell and hit my head. I woke up and I felt them flutter. I've been sitting here, trying to will them back inside of me."

"Okay." Dex raised his hand and slowly lowered it. "Breathe in then out. Take your time and think of something that brings you peace."

"I'll try." She inhaled and exhaled several times; her eyebrows were dipped low.

"You're still angry at me, aren't you?" Dex swallowed and relaxed his shoulders.

"I guess so." Yori turned her back to him.

Dex didn't move much. He just kept breathing in time with her, watching every move she made. Finally, her shoulders dropped, her arms relaxed at her sides, and the wings stopped their jumpy light show. Leisurely, they slid within her back and disappeared.

Yori started to jerk away.

"Don't. Not yet." He wanted to make sure she was calmer. Dex needed to tell her everything.

"Something else happened when I put Grady's ring on my finger. It was terrible. A nightmare that I was living, one that made me feel as though my skin was being ripped off of me. My core, my soul, seemed to be pulled from my body. It was pain like I never dreamed or imagined before. Something—or someone—was dragging me to a place by hooks they'd placed in my core."

"Oh, Dex, I..."

"My brother saw me in bed, and he brought my father to me. My dad was losing it and called in some of his friends. They helped me by teaching me the one secret weapon that we humans have to be free of the slavery of a Soul Warrior."

"Free?"

"It's being human, being protected by the creator all universes—all realms. Giving my allegiance and soul in allegiance to Him broke me free."

"Dex..."

"But there is a price. The ring left me with some of the residue of the changes even though my father was able to remove it. I don't know what he did with the ring. I only know that after that, he planned on us getting out of here. It didn't happen—for all of us."

Yori turned around. She wiped the tears from her eyes. "Thank you for sharing that with me." She ran to him and gave him a hug. "I was scared thinking about having to stay here alone or going back and not being able to act like nothing has changed."

Dex held his hands out to the side. He didn't want to make her feel uncomfortable. "Yori?"

She sniffled and lifted her gaze to his.

Dex cleared his throat. "Can I hug you back?"

Yori smiled. "Yes, and tightly, please."

Dex hugged her, nuzzling the top of her head, taking in the flowered scent of her hair, and realized he'd needed her hug as much as she'd needed his. He knew then they were ready to take on whatever was coming.

·22·

T hey packed some eggs and herbs for the rest of the journey. Dex followed closely behind Yori through the bush of the plush forest. He pushed past her to lead the way.

He missed being in the small home, but after they'd come to an understanding about their friendship, the tight quarters closed in on him. His heart had been interested in her since he first laid eyes on her, even after she'd rejected him the first time. He'd be her friend, but he couldn't offer her much more than that; it wouldn't be good for either of them. Problem was his heart and body didn't want to do the right thing. They were greedy. It was hard to force himself not to pull her to his body at night.

Since he kissed her, his lips trembled with the desire to do it again. It sucked. So, he decided not to let his eyes devour her as often as they did before. That's why he led the way through the bush. Using a thick firm branch to push the overgrown areas out of their way would take his mind off her beauty. He was in front so he didn't have to see her in the glimmering bikini of wing skin she wore. Torture. That's what it was.

"Dex, slow down. I don't know what to expect with this short cut."

He stopped but didn't turn around. "I want to beat the night. Vampires were in the woods near the skate park earlier this year. I caught London and some Soul Warriors fighting them." Dex didn't want to tell Yori the entire story behind that even though he'd never forget the video sent to him showing that Jake set her up for vampires to attack and kill her in those woods.

"I never liked that skate park." Yori came alongside him. "How you like my stick?" She lifted hers just above Dex's chest.

"Good size, thick enough to give you distance." Dex nodded as she lowered it.

"We have a good chance of beating the night if we can stay on this path. There is one direction the vamps won't go. We can cut through if we have to."

"You know these woods well?"

"I guess well enough. I memorized the map, but it was smudged in many places. Also, I never actually traveled these routes even though I know them by memory."

"So just drawing it over and over again helped you remember it?"

"Mostly, but my father always told a story as he walked me through each map. I started to associate the story with key locations that he wanted me to know, and my visual art interpretations always had drawn people that would act out a silly scene on the map. He insisted I draw it that way."

"Good memory technique. I'm going to use that if I get through high school alive."

"I heard a rumor. Kids that need to hide can get admitted into a special school."

"A rumor from whom?"

Yori shrugged. "This girl named Megan. She's like some undercover news reporter. She sends secret news messages that tell the truth of the strange things that go on here."

"Megan? The girl that sat in the back of our Art class

with orange hair?" Dex knew her. She'd sent him the video of London's death, but he didn't trust her at all.

"That's the one. Only for some reason, when I tried to share the information she gave me about her newsletter, the words got stuck in my mouth unless I spoke to someone that she'd sent news to before." Yori frowned.

Dex wondered about Megan at that time before he was willing to accept that strange things were happening around him. "She sent me news, nothing I wanted to see though."

Yori snorted. "It's never what you want to see. Did she ask you for a favor? A trade for the information?"

Dex considered her words and realized Megan hadn't asked him for anything. "Nope."

"Interesting. Maybe someone else paid for your subscription." Yori swatted away a hanging vine.

"I hope not. I think my youngest sister, Rei, was working for her." He didn't like that Rei had been friends with Megan; the girl gave him an uneasy feeling. He felt like she was a predator, as someone trained in fighting. Dex knew them well.

"Oh, that explains it. She was constantly paying; if you work for Megan, it's not easy. I bet she gave an oath of silence."

"What is Megan? Is she human? Do you know?" Dex wanted to make sure she was someone who could help; maybe they could find her and get help.

"I don't know for sure; I'd guessed she was human, but the fact that I couldn't spill the specifics about her small business of sharing news, giving favors, and asking for them, it's possible she wasn't."

There was rustling in the area ahead of them. Dex couldn't see anything since the forest was thick with low hanging branches, bushes, and thick grass.

"It's probably just a squirrel or rabbit. My father made sure I understood that the green parts of the forest were safe. The dying parts, not so much."

"I don't think I'll ever feel safe—anywhere. Least of all here." Dex made light of his confession by chuckling after. It didn't work though. It sounded like a wounded animal.

·23·

Besides the rustling noise further ahead, Dex didn't hear anything else. The sounds had stopped, and everything went still. It was unsettling him. The birds flew above but circled around without entering the space in front of them. It was as if the birds were afraid to go further.

"The birds aren't going forward. That's not a good sign." Dex stopped and lifted the stick he'd been using.

Yori lowered hers on top of his. "I've been in one dead spot of the forest, and literally nothing is alive in those places. We can pass through, I'm sure of it."

"Is this the only way to town?" Dex dropped his shoulders and turned around in the direction they came. "You can go back where it's safe."

"I'm not going back, Dex. We will make it. I can fight well enough to live and not use the pixie magic."

"Okay, stay close to me." Dex waved her alongside him. The hairs on his body rose on alert. He had to go on; he needed answers, and getting to town was the only way he was going to get them. It didn't stop his fear for Yori. He'd taught her to fight, but she held back since she was afraid of losing control.

They broke through the trees, and Dex's heart froze. In the dead space, the trees were barren of leaves. Their trunks were black with white pustules littering their bark. The trees hunched over with several inches of mud-splattered at the bases. The smell was like a wall of hot, rotted trash and infection. None of that bothered him as much as the frozen bodies caked in mud ahead of them.

There were several dozen forms in different ages, trapped in some type of frozen catatonic state. Their bodies bent and curved in unnatural forms, caked in thick brown mud to either conceal them or to consume them.

"Weird," Yori whispered. "All of them are covering their mouths and lower chins."

Dex raised a hand in front of Yori who stepped forward to investigate. He narrowed his gaze, hopping from one frozen figure to another. Their eyes were covered in mud too, but each and every one had covered their mouths with a hand, arm, or by their shirt.

"This is not good." Dex raised a hand to stop her.

"They could be statues. No one could stand that still without breathing, right? They are so caked with mud, it's hard to tell." Yori tapped Dex's leg with her stick. "We have to keep going. It's the only way."

"Are you sure? Have you come this way before?"

Yori sighed. "Never seen a dead place before. I didn't want to tell you, but the dead places move. They never stay in the same location. They just pop up...when conditions are right for them, I guess."

Dex bit his lower lip. "Let's go, be ready to fly away and leave me if you have to."

Yori shook her head. "I can't control it, and each time I use it, this grows." She pointed at the silver design sprouting from her temple since Nash manipulated her magic. "Showing that a change to full pixie could happen, and I'll never be able to get free of this place."

Dex pivoted toward her and laid his hands on her shoulders. "You use it. Promise me, or we will go back."

Yori held his gaze. "I will fight first, and if...the magic happens, it happens."

Dex released his breath. "I'll take that. C'mon." He lifted his finger to his lips and crouched low. He shaped a tight grasp on the thick stick as he eyed the frozen figures in front of them. He found the shortest path to the other side. It was through the middle of them. Dex decided that wasn't the best way and moved quietly along the outer perimeter of the strange circle of frozen people.

His hearing was keen. A slight cracking noise seized his attention. Dex didn't know if it was from the barren trees that littered the land or the frozen figures. Something was off. The hairs on his neck rose, and he felt like they were being watched. He shook off the feeling and reached back for Yori's hand. She didn't want to use her wings to get out of there, but Dex swore he'd make her use every trick she had to get free.

Dex concentrated on keeping his breathing steady. He stared at one then another of the bodies frozen in grotesque forms of pain and anguish. If this was art, the person had a sick sense of horror and talent for realism. Every one of them with their mouths covered by a hand, an arm, or another's body—except the rags they wore swayed from time to time. The eyes were closed in a grimace or half-open. Dex studied their bodies, looking for something to indicate whether they were real or statues. None of them even seemed to be breathing. He guessed that if they were only statues, he and Yori must have appeared crazy to be afraid of them. His instincts, though, warned him that there was a predator after them. It may not be the misshapen art of bodies they were working their way around, but something in this dead place was watching them. Dex spared a peek up at the tree branches reaching toward the sky. There was nothing in them. No birds, no leaves, no life.

"Almost there," Yori whispered next to him. "Maybe they are just statues after all."

Dex narrowed his eyes at one statue of a boy crouched low under another, and he could have sworn its eye moved. "Be ready for anything." He tightened his grasp on his stick. He was sweating and wiped his forehead with the back of his hand. Every muscle in his body was taut and ready to strike.

He picked up the pace and grabbed Yori's hand with his free one to help her along since his stride was much longer than hers. Dex was glad she didn't complain, but he heard her labored breathing as she practically jogged to keep up with him. He wanted out of there. A small path covered in damp leaves and mud led through the group of still figures.

"Almost there." Dex reached the mouth of the ominous brush of bristled trees. They curved over with thick leaves and thorns, making a black and brown branch-tunnel. "There's light coming through the tunnel."

"That's a good sign the dead space is finished there."

Dex held Yori's wrist then moved his hand to envelop hers. Her fingers enclosed around his, and a tingling raced up his arm. The first touch like this since their kiss. Friendship. That's what he had to remind himself he was fighting to survive this for, her friendship.

At the mouth of the tunnel, Dex pushed her in front of him and pivoted around one last time, he hoped. He swore the statues were closer than before. With a shake of his head, Dex followed Yori into the tree-tunnel.

·24·

The tunnel was dark except for the glow of the light from the other side. It was like a cast of light from the sun. The branches swayed and bent as though imitating cracking their knuckles. The smell was of damp rotted wood, and the moistness in the air cooled Dex's heated skin. He kept an eye on the exit as Yori dragged her stick alongside her.

He refused to turn around to make sure the statues didn't follow them inside. Dex walked faster, but not so fast Yori had to run behind him. The further they ventured into the tunnel, the darker it got. He seemed to feel it as a presence at his back.

When they broke through the end of the tunnel, Dex relaxed and exhaled. They were in a small clearing with a rounded area of dead leaves and mud surrounded by green lush forest. Dex chuckled at the fear that had laced his blood on the trek through the dead part of the forest. He dropped his stick; no need for it since they were close to safety. The plush olive landscape was only a few yards away.

"Wait!" Yori tugged at Dex's wrist. "Someone is there." She pointed. "At the tree in the middle."

The tree rose about forty feet tall. At the base stood a small-statured girl. The thick trunk partially hid her body from sight. She was hunched over with her arms crossed and leaning on the trunk. Her shoulders bounced as though she was sobbing, but no sound came out in their direction.

Hair the color of wheat hung in long full strands that covered her face. Torn clothing hung from her thin frame.

"Don't go near her. It could be a trap." Dex spent a moment assessing whether anything was different about the girl.

"She's crying." Yori frowned back at him and tapped her stick to the ground.

Dex slowly squatted to grasp his stick. He walked in front of Yori, putting up a staying hand and moving closer. "Hey, are you alright?" His heart beat faster. He didn't feel good about this. The girl didn't lift her face. Why not?

Slowly, her head moved, and he could see a sliver of her pale forehead. He crept closer. The girl's sniffling stopped. Dex hesitated then dipped his eyebrows together as Yori moved up next to him. He waved her away, pointing his stick diagonal to the now-quiet girl.

The girl's black slanted eyes watched him, unblinking. Predatory. He could only see her eyes; her arm still covered the bridge of her nose and below. Asian? That's the first assumption Dex made, although he couldn't decipher her nationality from where he stood.

Dex let out the air from his stomach and took a step closer to the girl. "It's alright." He held up the palm of his hand. "We can help."

She narrowed her eyes.

A low growl escaped from her. The girl leaped at him. His jaw dropped. He whipped the stick at her unfurled claws. Her nose was grotesque as was the lower portion of her face. Her jaws were scrunched in and crowded with pin-sharp teeth. The girl-beast moved with quickness, dodging each of his blocks but still unable to come close. She lunged, and Dex flexed his stick up to wedge in her teeth. He kicked her leg, and she smoothly hopped onto the other. He whacked downward on her head, and she jerked out of the way. Her sharp nails sliced at him. Dex punched her then elbowed her in the stomach. He didn't hold back any of his barely known abilities; he acted on instinct.

"Dex! More...from the tunnel!" Yori screamed. She frantically whacked her stick at a few between her yelps.

"Get over here! Behind me, back to back." Dex parried away from a slash of the creature's claws.

He turned once Yori's back touched his. He had to get her out of there. Dex pivoted. Kicked a creature flying through, reaching for him, and grasped Yori at the waist. Dex picked up her light form and threw her with all the strength he had. "Fly away! Go!"

Her wings sprouted. A sharp pain tore at his shoulder. The slant-eyed creature was on his shoulder, ripping his skin. It burned, and it ticked him off. Something was fighting its way into his veins; his body tried to reject it. Fire traveled through his body. The heat fueled his determination to get out of there alive.

A burst of power deep within his stomach sprang forth, energizing within him. A creature charged. He back-kicked the male charging creature while swiping his stick at another, breaking it. The girl's teeth dug deeper. Her slight legs wrapped around him. She was settling in for a good meal.

Dex punched one creature. Another leaped at him. He bent and stabbed part of the broken branch through it. Its razor-sharp teeth sank into his arm as it yanked the stick from his flesh. Dex had doubts he would survive. The girl's bite was weakened, but another sank into his other shoulder. Dex fought but felt sluggish. He was losing blood. Too much. His vision blurred. He stumbled, now with two biters on his shoulders and another on each of his legs.

"Yori..." he uttered, praying she'd kept going—that his death wouldn't be for nothing.

Dex elbowed another. Blood dripped down his face as a creature bit his ear. He kicked one away. The growls were hungry and animalistic.

He groaned as another sharp bite pricked the top of his head. Dex pushed on, dragging the creatures with him as he fell to the side. Maybe, if he could just get to the green healthy part of the forest, he would survive. So many of the creature's bit at his skin Dex wondered how their thin bodies had crowded in on him so fast. Almost...there. So sleepy. Pain, too much burning pain. Darkness, it was his long-time friend, and with every part of his body throbbing in pain, he welcomed it.

·25·

Dex felt lighter. He must be dreaming of being alive. If he was dreaming, why did he feel so sore? He'd lost the fight. He sucked. His father wouldn't have let him hear the end of it. Maybe if he stayed asleep, he'd be back in his mind to New York, waking up to tag walls of abandoned buildings with his artwork. He would go to school where he'd dodge first period homeroom to meet up with his best friends, who ditched him the last time they tagged the train and got caught.

"Dex! Dexter! Wake up," Yori called. "Get off of him. Oof!"

Dex smacked his teeth and raised his hand to his head. God help him. His eyelids were so heavy. He bucked, pushing off the hot dead weight of something that felt like a female.

"Ah!" Yori screamed. "What are you?"

Dex jerked up, forcing his eyes open. His hands unconsciously moved to his neck and then his chest. He stared at the girl who'd lured them with her fake cries. He swayed at the grogginess, blinking away while releasing a deep stream of air. His body throbbed, not with pain but with some sort of healing ache. It was an itchiness deep within that brought the ache of healing. He bent his legs, put his hands down to brace himself, and tensed. Dex was ready to counter an attack. The once misshapen girl now had the smooth skin of a normal person.

"Wait!" the girl lifted a hand. "I'm healed. I won't hurt you." The girl shied away from Yori's raised stick.

With a surge of energy, Dex hopped to his feet. He stepped in front of Yori to face the girl. Her almond eyes appeared calm. She scratched her small blood covered nose then wiped her forearm across stained lips.

Dex lunged at her; it was his blood. Bluish red. She was fast, but Dex was faster. He grabbed her tattered shirt. "You bit me!"

The girl nodded. "Yes, but I was rabid." She lifted a hand and touched his face almost like a caress. "You saved me. I was diseased and couldn't shift back to either human or my animal. It was horrible." Her voice had a sultry lisp to it. She leaned in, sniffing him.

Dex dropped her. "So now I'm rabid?" A shiver rocketed up his spine.

"No. You healed me; the others bit me then were healed too. In rabid form, you are drawn most to other shifters. I attacked you since I was starving and you were the only non-diseased person I'd seen in ages. Once you cured me, each shifter bitten by a healed one was healed and so on." The girl lifted a tattered sleeve. "See?" Bite marks scarred her.

"Why didn't the bites completely heal?" Dex eyed her arm, prepared to beat her down again if he had to. Yori tensed. He lifted a staying hand to her.

"I don't think they will. I heal fast, even faster than when I was rabid. The problem was I couldn't completely shift to either human or animal. I was something in-between and hungry to the point of starving. Nothing I attacked staved the hunger. It was like starving, going crazed, and watching it from a sane mind but unable to control your own insanity." The girl moved fast, snatched his ripped shirt down his shoulder. "You aren't marked."

Dex felt Yori's lighter touch behind him. "You don't have a scar on you." Her stick lifted and poked the girl's shoulder. "Dex, you had fourteen of them gnawing on you." Yori jumped back.

The girl studied him. "Are you a Soul Warrior? They had the magic to heal us but killed my kind instead."

Dex shook his head. "No. I'm nothing like them."

"Tell me, what species are you?" The girl walked around him, her eyes scanning him from head to toe. "You appear human, smell human, but you have something extra in you." She closed her eyes, wrapped an arm around him. Putting her nose at the base of his neck, she sniffed deeper. "Oh, I see what you are."

Dex pried her from around his neck and pushed her away. He crossed his arms. "What's your name?"

"Izume. I am Princess to the leopard shifter nation." Her chin lifted. "At least the ones here in the Void." She sighed. "While hunting with my brother, I was attacked." Izume lowered her head. "Then infected the others along with me."

"The Soul Warriors imprisoned some of you?" Dex asked, not wanting to give away that he knew what happened to the ones captured.

"They did. The king of this void doesn't like those who test his power—or the power of his twelve enforcers. My father... He did and disappeared. Our search for him didn't end well."

"What did you mean when you said you see who I am?" Dex wanted to know about what he had become. He was discovering it but needed to know he was changing to be better, not enslaved by dark magic.

Izume smiled. "That, you shall come to know on your own. I am forever indebted to you."

"You don't have to be. We should help others when we can. I am glad it didn't lead to my death."

"Death won't come easy to you. There is too much for you to do for us all here. Where are you going? I know these woods; it gets more dangerous the closer you get to town. Unless you know the way of the unknowns."

"What does that mean?" Dex pinched his chin.

"There are those who are living a lie in this world. They chose to play out the fantasy of a life that mirrors the Earth Realm. We shifters don't; we live in the hidden world of this place and are considered the unknowns."

"Are only shifters living that way?" Yori asked. "I heard of a school where people who aren't able to live in the city can hide and try to live a normal life."

Izume smiled. "Oh, there are many who live the life of unknowns, but when we are discovered, the Soul Warriors police us, kill us, or use us for their experiments."

"I want to be an unknown." Yori tapped her stick on the ground. Her wings fluttered before sinking slowly into her skin. "Or go to the Earth Realm."

Izume gave her a sanguine gaze. "But you are pixie-human. They are able to conceal their wings, which means they can go undetected around magicals. Extremely rare. If they learn who you are... They will never allow you to leave, especially when they realize what they can use you for."

"I've got her. No one will hurt her." Dex stepped in front of Yori. "I'm going to town."

"Hmmm, I see." She pouted then smacked her teeth. "I will guide you through a safe passage and protect you while doing so." She morphed into a huge, gold, spotted leopard. *Follow me, and keep your pixie-human under control.*

Dex laid a hand on Yori's shoulder. "Close your mouth."

Yori swallowed. Her wings extended from their hiding place in her back and fluttered. "Ah...oh," she whispered and lifted her hand to cover her mouth. His heart twitched at her loss of words. He wanted to kiss her, pull her close to him, and tell her he was falling in love with her, but that was a bad idea. She was right to keep him in the friend zone because as much as he wanted her, Dex didn't want to devour her with his baggage.

He didn't know what his blood contained, but if he could heal rabid shifters, he needed to find the exact capabilities of a Vigilant.

·26·

Dex could now see in the dark. What the hell had happened to him? Did her bite, the multiple bites of the shifters, change him even more? He didn't know and was too afraid to ask Izume. Her leopard form sauntered languidly through the dark forest where small animals moved out of her way. The forest was thick. And dark—dense leaves all around blocked the moonlight. Yori allowed him to hold her hand, probably because she couldn't see where she was going...

"Step over the dead log." Dex placed his hands on her hips and lifted her over. Yori shivered within his hands, and he hoped it didn't mean that she was uncomfortable with his touch.

The fallen leaves gave a soft crunch under their feet. Nocturnal animals scurried and hid as they drew closer.

"How much further is it?" Yori whispered.

Dex waited, wondering what to say to Izume but remained silent.

"I don't know; she's not hurrying." Dex pointed at Izume.

"I'm in no hurry to get you to the city of danger. I can't follow you there. At least not on the streets." Izume released a low growl.

Dex didn't repeat what Izume told him. "We'll get there."

Yori hesitated; her hand went slack within his. He ignored it and tightened his grasp around hers. "Do you trust her?"

He glanced at Izume.

Izume slowed as if waiting for his answer.

"I do."

"Can you communicate with her animal?" Yori's hand squeezed his.

"Do not tell her," Izume warned, but her pace didn't falter.

"I am observant," Dex responded. *How are you able to communicate with me?*

You were bitten by multiple in my tribe. This is usually done in a ceremony to transition a human when a shifter meets their life-mate and desires to have children with them. The only way a shifter babe can be born to a human is to infect them with our magic. We can control the release of magic that gives the human long life and some of our qualities – but when rabid, we can control nothing of our nature. The Soul Warriors' magic changes their human DNA, therefore they can't partake in this no matter how many of the rabid shifters bite them. You, well, you are much different. It is your humanity that has saved you and created something quite powerful. Powerful enough to frighten the Overlord to this place.

"Do you know how to find Detective Whalen?" Yori whispered.

Izume froze at Yori's words. Dex stopped. "I do. Many times I approached to ask him questions, but each time, I turned around and left. It felt like I was betraying my father. My dad didn't want me to talk to the detective, especially after the guy blackmailed him."

"What? Why would he do that?" Yori's hand moved up to his forearm.

"Detective Whalen wanted to use me, without my knowledge, to be recruited by the elite on the football team."

"You knew what they were, didn't you?"

"Not at the time, but I do now. They were the Soul Thieves in training. The head coach of the varsity team was the main recruiter. He's high in the organization. Apparently, I was set up from the start, the house, the neighborhood, and the school. That's how they got to Trey. He and I officially talked to each other for the first time at one of the ceremonies."

"I don't know. It could be really dangerous for us to go back." Yori stopped walking and dropped Dex's hand.

She is correct. They may have their slaves looking for you. The twelve enforcers have creatures of duality working for them. If they have your scent, you may alert them.

"I will be fine." Dex patted Izume's back. *Don't I smell different now that your people altered me?*

If a leopard could chuckle, that's what the noise Izume made sounded like. *Right. You do smell different. If you need help from other shifters, speak through telepathy, and use my name. But be careful, not all shifters are friendly, especially to us 'unknown' since the twelve are all shifters in power and we are a challenge to their power.*

Yori allowed Dex to re-grasp her hand. "If you are sure seeking Detective Whalen is worth it, I can send a message to Megan. She is powerful and can help us. She is the center of an underground news organization. Megan makes things happen."

"Megan? How would you contact her?" He waved a hand. "Didn't I mention that I don't trust her at all?" Dex remembered the redheaded minx clearly: intelligent and predatory eyes. He didn't want to give her any information to use against him. "Don't tell her anything about me or mine—ever." The last time he was contacted by Megan, she sent him a video of London being murdered. That was something he'd never forget. Even before then, he'd felt her tracking him. No, he didn't want to have anything to do with Megan. He turned to Yori and grabbed the stick in her hand. "Promise me you won't tell Megan anything."

Yori sighed. "I won't."

He peered at the field near the edge of the woods. It had well-manicured grass and could be a practice field for soccer, lacrosse, or kickball. He saw it framed between the trees bordering the woods. Izume stood behind him trying to conceal herself.

"We need to wait until dark to get to the police station. He works nights mostly, and it's a mile walk through the city." A track team on the field was running sprints. Dex wondered how long before they would leave. He didn't want to run into anyone. "Especially since we don't have any money."

Izume partially transformed and came to stand between him and Yori. "I am happy to be of small service to you. I know of another of our kind who may happen upon the field beyond the woods. He will smell you out, recognize my scent on you, and help." She kissed his cheek.

Dex stepped back and lifted his eyebrows at her. Izume was covered in fur, but her human form was revealed...with the exception of her leopard ears and nose. She reminded him of one of the actors he'd seen at the play his mother and sisters dragged him to called *Cats*.

"I have money for you. We keep it under some of the rocks at the many exits just in case one of our kind needs it when they breach the city."

"Thanks for offering it."

Izume smiled at him. She invaded his space, sniffed him, and laid her hand on his chest.

Dex heart twitched at the frown on Yori's face. She recovered and relaxed, turning away from them.

"She is jealous." Izume smirked. "It can work in your favor."

"That's not what I want." He stepped back from Izume. "I need you to find my sister or my brother. They were taken. Ask anyone you know if they have information."

Izume studied him, crossing her arms. "I will see what I can do. My brother is on the other side. He works for them as a runner."

"Thanks, you owe me no debt, but I will appreciate anything you can do to help them—to help me."

"Be careful. When a person disappears from the city, all are supposed to forget them." Izume grasped his chin. "You are supposed to stay gone."

Dex chuckled. "You see, trying to do what I'm supposed to do didn't work that well for me. So, I think I am going to just do what I want. Own it. Because, I need answers, and I need to save my family."

Izume nodded and caressed his cheek. "I will do what I can to find them for you. As for her, I see love in her eyes," Izume whispered, close enough to kiss him. "Sadly, she's too afraid to grasp it... If only you and I could have..." She dropped her hand. "I hope she finds her way to you." She transformed and ran through the thick brush.

Dex crossed his arms, his gaze turning away from the leopard shifter that unknowingly gave him a great gift. She thought Yori loved him, and whether Yori did or not, the fact that another confirmed some connection between them gave him hope. Dex regretted that she was afraid of falling in love, thanks to Jake. Crap, he was too. Only, he had nothing else, no one else. What they'd been through together was too insane to share with anyone—ever. He'd thought he loved London, but now he realized the love they shared was flawed. It wasn't built on trust, friendship, or sacrifice. London never felt he was strong enough to protect her—or carry the weight of her trust. He understood why now. He just didn't want to admit it.

Dex felt Yori's tentative presence behind him. "We have hours until it gets dark enough to go on the streets."

"I know. Even so, it may not be safe if they still have the curfew in effect. Police will be patrolling, and we don't want to be stopped. We can search for the money Izume said would be under a rock."

Yori laughed. "She didn't give you a better clue? I thought she liked you, really liked you. Yori pointed at the numerous rocks scattered between the trees and in the grass around them. There were even more at the bases of the bushes that bordered the woods as a preliminary barrier and warning to any that would want to enter.

"C'mon, she didn't like me that much. Besides, I like someone else." Dex leveled Yori with a stare. "A lot."

She bit her lip. Yori squatted in front of a rock. "We may as well look since we have some daylight."

Dex didn't need daylight to see, but telling Yori that new fact about him would worry her. He sat next to her and turned over a few rocks. Nothing was under them but dirt. He sniffed, realizing that he could smell the damp dirt under each rock before he lifted it. Maybe another shifter trait was keen smell. He imagined the scent of copper and the ink on a dollar. While Yori randomly picked up rocks, he concentrated, using his nose to guide him. Dex walked through the trees, close to a random bush, and it hit him. The smell of copper, ink, and Izume. He crouched next to an odd-shaped stone, laying a palm on it. Part of it was raised in the shape of a small circular symbol. Dex tried to understand the symbol and remembered the image Izume placed in his mind before she left. It must be a symbol for her tribe. He lifted it, and there was a leather satchel. Dex shook it. Coins jingled within it. He opened it. Cash. He sat on the ground and counted out the twenties, fives, and one-dollar bills. The satchel held about five hundred dollars in cash and four dollars in coins. Dex took a hundred dollars. He placed the rest of it back in the satchel. He stuffed the bag under the rock then headed back toward Yori who was still picking up and placing down the rocks the way she'd found them.

"I got the money."

"I turned over fifty rocks, and you did only a quarter of that. How are you so lucky?" Yori stomped her foot while lifting one side of her lip.

Dex shrugged. "I just looked in a different section." He sat on the soft ground and tugged Yori by the arm to sit on one of the larger rocks. It put them face to face. "Are you ready for this?" He pushed deep the hunger he felt at wanting to kiss her, hoping to cover his desire to move out of her friend zone. "The journey."

Yori pursed her lips and picked a berry from the bush at the base of a nearby tree. "I am." She popped it in her mouth. "I'm just tired, and I want to be safe."

"I get that. I do too." He couldn't help his desire to test her, touch her. Dex traced her hand with his finger. "You're a good friend. Thanks for trying to save me back there even though I wanted you to get to safety."

Yori slouched her shoulders. Her hand trembled under his, but she didn't move away. "I stayed hidden a long time. I just watched, and...I am sorry I couldn't find a way to stop their attack. They wouldn't stop coming for you. The creatures changed from monsters with huge jagged, bloody teeth and clawed fingers to humans. They fell to the ground and convulsed, they just collapsed until I thought they'd died. After a few minutes, they awakened like they'd come out of some trance. They tried moving Izume but left when I made a tree fall." She sighed. "I should've tried harder to hold myself together and help you."

Dex's jaw dropped. He quickly recovered, trying to relax. "Don't feel that way. You did what I asked." He raised an eyebrow at her comment about making a tree fall. He didn't want to question her too much about that. Likely, her magic reacted to her distress.

Yori placed her finger on top of his. "It was the hardest thing I've ever had to do." She lifted her eyes to his; there was a war going on within them.

Dex smiled. His heart beat rapidly as he understood the tentative touch of her finger. Dex hesitated since she was trying to resist the pull between them, but he didn't want her to. He entwined his fingers with hers then tugged her toward him. Dex gently rested a hand on her shoulder. He slowly moved it up to her neck. His heart thundered in his chest; he felt like it would be ripped from him if she denied him. He was starving for her. The comfort, the softness, the acceptance of a friend—a love.

"Can I kiss you?" His voice was raspy and low. Dex gazed at her, willing her with all he had in him to say yes.

"Please do." Yori closed her eyes.

Dex pressed his lips softly to hers, waiting. He savored the trembling when touching Yori's. His mouth watered at the thought of consuming the essence of her sweetness if she'd just let him taste a bit more of it. He waited for her to give him a sign she was ready to open and let him in. Within a few moments, she unraveled. Yori moaned and kissed him back hungrily. Dex matched her desperation, sliding her off the rock and into his lap. He wrapped her within his arms and rocked her before pulling away. Every hair on his body lifted at attention, he'd better back off before pushing too far.

Resting his forehead on hers, Dex calmed his heavy breathing and the rush of his rapid heartbeat. "You are the best friend I've ever had." He smiled and slid a shaking hand up the curve of her jaw to delve into the mass of curls that framed her neck.

"You are mine too," she whispered.

Dex wanted to kiss away the dampness that teased her lashes; he prayed they were tears of joy. He'd only ever wanted to make her feel safe and wanted by him.

·28·

Dex held her there for a moment until he knew the intensity of his stare was too much for her. Yori rested her head in the curve of his shoulder.

"Dex, I don't think it's smart of me to fall for you, but I can't help myself. I'm scared." Yori started to pull away.

"I'm scared too." He rubbed her arm and snuggled her back into his embrace. "Guys have feelings, and being rejected hurts like hell. But, in life you have to take risks, right? I'd rather take that risk on you than anyone else. We deserve to get whatever happiness we can grab right now. If we waste it, what will I hold onto when things go to hell again?"

Yori sighed. "I've had so many disappointments even though I try to think of the good things. I hope one day I can have a normal life, at least one where I don't have to worry about anything but homework, the prom, and grades. I don't trust myself to make the right decisions. I've made so many mistakes about friends, love...everything."

"I try to learn from mine. What have you learned about me? I won't be a mistake for you." He put his thumb under her chin to catch her attention.

Yori inhaled, slowly blinking as if thinking about what she was about to say, "You are a fighter. You never give up on those you care about, but Dex...you were friends with Soul Thieves. That's a bad group of friends to have; they will kill you or indoctrinate you. I don't want to go through that again with anyone. I almost died because of the evil of that dark magic."

"I'm not a product of friendships or influences of others. Give me some credit in owning my screw-ups."

Yori smiled. "I will do that." Her shoulders dropped. "I just want a normal life at the end of this."

Dex laughed. "We want the same things. Let me help make that happen. After I find my family, we can go back to school like nothing's happened."

Yori groaned. "We've already missed the beginning of school. I can't repeat the eleventh grade."

"I know; that would be brutal." Dex scratched his chin. The guys he'd seen on the field through the woods were gone. Dusk dimmed the landscape. "What school was that out there?"

"Arcane High School. Their teams compete to get into the same leagues as ours. Their coaches don't have the same influence as the coaches at our school. The kids at Arcane appear normal-sized, not super-sized like the guys on our football team. They are the runts in the choices for the elite recruiters, so basically the Soul Thieves don't bother with scouting them. I think the Overlord probably waits to see if they have kids who will be able to cross over. Evil is patient here."

Dex nodded. He studied the field in front of them. "We have to go. I need new clothes. I look and smell like a dead animal."

Yori pinched her nose. "You said it, so do I." She got off his lap and stretched.

Dex hopped up and ripped off the dingy barely there t-shirt. "Maybe someone left behind some clothes."

Yori grasped his arm. "I can...um, maybe make you some clothes and clean you up."

"You sure? I don't want to be turned into a toad or something." Dex rubbed his upper chest. "But if you can help me with this stink and some clothes, it will be safer for us."

"I've been practicing...when I couldn't sleep. On myself and the trees. I thought maybe if I could control it more...." Yori pursed her lips to the side.

"I don't want you using the magic. It'll make you turn darker." Dex traced the silver tattoo that now extended from her temple to her cheek. It was a beautiful accent to her brown skin. Dex studied her for a moment; he didn't want her to change into something else. "You know, your human side has power too. We don't need magic. Let's use our minds and logic instead." He leaned in and kissed her. "And you...have a beautiful mind."

"You're right. I don't want to risk it." She sighed and placed her hand on his. "It's grown hasn't it?"

"No, it just got a little thicker. Do you feel different?" Dex didn't know how to stop this change in her; they needed answers.

"I feel the same." Yori placed her other hand on her heart. "At least here I do."

Dex lifted a side of his lips. "That's all that matters. Now let's go to the field and see if anyone left something behind."

29

He led the way. It was dusk, and the players on the field had been gone for a little while. Thick trimmed grass and benches lined one side. Dex missed this, sports and nothing but high school drama. These kids didn't know they were living in a dream—a fake reality—and that dark sinister creatures awaited their trek through the woods.

"Over here, on the benches." Dex pivoted, hoping for any piece of clothing left behind. First, he wanted to cover Yori's lush body. Although she was petite, she had nicely shaped hips and full breasts he wanted to cover up. The weather was cooler on the field.

"I will just add more to this." Yori extended the multi-colored shorts down her legs and up her torso.

"Okay." Dex stared at her new form-fitted outfit. It made her appear even sexier than before, but he held his comment, not wanting to embarrass her. He turned and jogged to a bench at the far end where he'd seen something on the ground.

Dex slid to a stop. He bent to pick up a discarded shirt and sweatpants. The pounding of running feet startled him. Looking up, he stood to face the kid whose clothes he held in his hand.

The blond boy in a t-shirt and shorts stopped in front of him. "Hey! That's my stuff."

"I'm sorry. I tore my shirt in the woods and thought no one wanted these."

The guy put his hands on his hips, bending a bit as he caught his breath. "It's okay. You look like you need them more than I do."

"I appreciate it. Can, I uh..." Dex hated asking for help, but if this kid could give them a ride, it would save them some time. "...ask you for a ride?"

The guy narrowed his eyes then bent at the waist to peep at Yori. "She with you?"

"Yeah, my girlfriend and I." Dex sighed. "You know... never mind. Thanks for the clothes though."

The guy shook his head. "No, I can give you a ride. My name's Milo. It's just...you can never be too careful." He looked over his shoulder as though checking to see if any of his teammates were watching. He turned back to Dex. He smiled and held out his hand. "I'm able to give you a ride. I wanted to make sure no one saw us. My teammates can be assholes to people they see need help. Great guys but rough around the edges."

Dex shook his hand. "I appreciate the help." He released it to put on the t-shirt and sweatpants.

"I have some jeans you can fit and shoes. I basically live out of my car." Milo shrugged. "This way." He waved and started walking.

Dex called to Yori. "He's good. Let's go."

She jogged up next to him. Dex held out his hand for her. He wanted Milo to know Yori was taken. He wasn't in the mood to have his girlfriend flirted with, especially since he never formally asked her to be his.

She grasped his hand and placed her other farther up on his arm. His chest pressed outward. Dex hoped Milo was a good guy; he didn't feel like fighting tonight.

Dex followed their new friend to the parking lot on the other side of the field—deserted except for a beat-up blue Jeep.

"The door is open." Milo pressed the key fob in his hand and opened the driver's side door.

Dex nodded at a hesitant Yori then got in the car. She slid into the back and crossed her arms.

"Nice car."

"I got it a month ago. I saved a ton of money working overtime at the movie theater." Milo laughed and started the engine. "I don't think I ever want to smell popcorn again."

"I can imagine." Dex clicked on his seatbelt.

"Where to?"

Taking a moment to think about what was near the police station where Detective Whalen worked, he remembered the Ice Cream Shack that he'd avoided after the detective arrested him.

"Uh, the Ice Cream Shack." Dex put his hands on his thighs.

"Closed down a month ago." Milo cleared his throat. "Look, I have lived here a while, and I know anyone that comes from the woods is either running or never want to go back. I want to help you. I do. If you'd let me."

Dex frowned. "How can you help me?"

"First, I'll take you somewhere to eat near the Ice Cream Shack." He pulled down his visor and grabbed a card that fell out. "This is a friend. She's weird but knows how to help people. It's always a price with her but something you can pay."

The card looked familiar, similar to the one that he'd used to discover what happened to his former girlfriend. It didn't end well. He hesitated.

Milo pushed it toward him. "Food first, and call her if you want."

Dex grasped the card from him and swore it shocked him. He almost dropped it. Instead, he tucked it in the pocket of his pants. "Thanks. I'll take you up on the food."

"Good, you won't regret it. There's nothing like a good meal."

"Yeah." Dex swallowed; it felt like the card was burning a hole in his pants, trying to coerce him to read it. He wouldn't. Not until he had no other options.

30

They'd passed the police station about two blocks back. Dex wanted to tell Milo to stop, but he was too hungry to argue. They pulled into a diner bearing a blazing sign that said *Breakfast All Day*.

"Don't be fooled by the sign. They have good burgers and burritos too." Milo parked. "My father owns the place and feeds me and my friends for free, so don't feel like you have to pay me back for the meal." He stopped the car.

"Thanks. Really, I appreciate this." Dex dug in his pocket for some cash. "But let me at least pay for your gas."

"Nope. Someone helped me like I'm helping you. I am returning the favor."

"Thanks, Milo, we both are hungry." Yori leaned up from the backseat and waved at Dex to hurry.

He scrambled out of the car, feeling uncomfortable with Milo's kindness. So much had happened to them that it was hard to believe someone was being genuine. He didn't sense anything off with Milo. The guy's scent was fresh and calm and shifter-like. Dex was willing to wait to learn if Milo was trustworthy or not.

Milo pushed through the door. He held it open for Dex and Yori.

There was only an elderly couple, one cop, and a woman with two kids in the diner.

"Hey, Beth, can you get me my usual times three and

bring it to the booth over there?" Milo called to the lady behind the counter at the bar.

"No problem. I'll have the new girl do it." The older lady turned away from them and went behind the back counter to the kitchen.

Dex took several breaths and flexed his fingers to relax before following the others to the booth on the far side of the diner. It was tucked away so that no one who walked in would see them if they weren't looking for them. Dex was starting to think Milo wasn't so bad.

Dex took the seat facing the door and window and motioned for Yori to sit next to the wall. He wanted to be ready in case things didn't go well.

Milo sat facing them and waved the girl over. The brown-haired girl barely looked at the other two as she stared at Milo with what seemed like awe.

"Milkshakes, cheese fries, corn on the cob, and the burgers are coming up in a minute," the girl squeaked. She placed a basket of fries, waters, and chicken tenders on the table.

Milo took some of the plates and put them in the middle of the table. The girl scurried away.

Dex grabbed one of the wet wipes the girl dropped on the table, and Yori took one also. He was a bit embarrassed by how dirty his hands were.

Milo grabbed some fries and stuffed them in his mouth. Dex joined in and did the same while Yori took one at a time.

"So..." Milo grabbed a glass of water and gulped it down with his food. "What's your story?"

Dex shrugged. "No story, really."

"What school you go to?" Milo relaxed back against the booth's cushioned seat.

"Not in school. Taking a year off to think about what I want to do next." Dex took a few fries, his hand touched Yori's lightly, and he adjusted his hand to allow her to grab a chicken tender.

The waitress came, and Dex moved his hands while she placed the burgers, cheese fries, and milkshakes on the table. "Anything else?" The girl glanced at Yori and Dex. She turned and leaned toward Milo.

"This is good. Thanks...uh?"

"Greta, I forgot to put on my nametag."

"Yeah, Greta, I'll let you know when we need refills, okay?"

"Sure." The girl left but glanced back at Milo with an adoring smile.

Dex chuckled. "She likes you."

"Most of the new waitresses do. I guess because I am related to the owner. It doesn't mean I have any money though." Milo laughed. "So, back to the story. You are drop-outs trying to figure out what you want to do with your life?"

Dex frowned. "We are not drop-outs."

"It's complicated," Yori added.

Milo nodded slowly. "I get it. You don't want to share. Well, about me then." He wiped his hands against one another. Milo licked his lips and grabbed his burger. "I'm the youngest of five, the runt of the family, but about three years ago, my father called in a favor for me to transfer from Arcane High School to Purview Academy. You ever play football?"

"Some." Dex bit his burger. It was so good he had to force himself not to stuff it in his mouth like a starved beast.

"You should. You have the size and the look." Milo shrugged. "Anyway, I love the sport, but my body isn't made for it. I do better with lacrosse, and Purview Academy has a gold standard team there."

"What about your siblings?" Yori piled more chicken tenders and cheese fries on her plate.

"My brothers are grown, and you can say they got off easy. I haven't seen them since we moved here." Milo's expression turned dark. "And my sister that moved with us, she went missing the month we got here."

"You've been here how long? There was a rumor of a serial killer. I think there was curfew or something." Dex finished off his burger. He fought the urge to lick his fingers. He pinched several the cheese fries between his fingers and stuffed them in his mouth.

"This was after the undercover newsletter I got concluded that case was closed. The killer was put to sleep." Milo leaned forward and whispered, "Just like she promised would happen."

Dex frowned and froze. "Who promised?"

Milo pointed downward. "The lead on the card I gave you. Sometimes they make predictions or promises to end crimes that can't be solved. You can pay them to find people, right a wrong for you. I did it, but...nothing's come of it yet."

"Why would you tell us this?" Dex lifted the fry. He leaned forward and tossed it onto the table. "You don't know me."

Milo smiled. "No, but I can smell you. You have the scent of someone from my tribe. You came from the secret passage. I know I can trust you."

"You're a shifter?" Yori whispered.

"I am, but no one knows that we are. My sister went to meet her boyfriend in the woods and never came back."

"Your sister was probably infected. There was an

outbreak. They were called 'sago' rabid shifters. Many of them were...captured." Dex sighed. "I'm sorry."

Milo rubbed a hand down his face. "That's more than I knew or could have guessed from what I gathered through various sources."

"When was the last time you saw anyone from your tribe?" Dex was gauging how long he'd been gone.

"It had been a year. My sister went missing soon afterward." Milo balled his fists and rubbed them on the table.

"I know how it is." Dex put his elbows on the table. "There's a detective who can help."

Milo snorted. "They are all corrupt. You don't know how things work here, but the new chief of police is a minion of the twelve. They use detectives to hunt people who ask too many questions and to keep the sleeping public in the illusion of safety. No thanks. I'll do things my way."

"Understood. Well, if you don't mind, we better go." Dex moved from the seat. He tossed a few bills on the table. "Give that to Greta." He held out a hand for Yori.

She grasped it and stood next to him. "Thanks, Milo."

"Anytime. If you need to find me, come here, go to the shed in the back. You want my cellphone number?"

"Nah, I don't have a phone."

"I'll leave my spare there for you if you want it, and some clothes."

"Thanks." Dex held up a hand to stop Milo from following them. "Really. I needed a friend, and you were that. I won't forget it."

Greta came around the corner toward them. She was looking down as she balanced the tray she was holding.

Dex tugged Yori out of Greta's way and headed to the door. If he ever saw Izume again, he would thank her. He'd

143

thought her attack was the death of him, but instead, it had been a gift of belonging he hadn't felt in a long time.

·31·

Dex didn't know if Detective Whalen was at the police station. All they had was hope. He considered going back to Milo's place: the shed, to wash up. But he wanted to know where to find the detective first. Quite a few cops were coming and going inside the building. It was busier than he'd thought a precinct could be.

He slowed before crossing the street toward the entrance. Yori grasped his forearm. "They would know you, but maybe I can ask for him. I look different than before. Besides, no one may be looking for me."

"How do you know? Nash told me they knew you were a pixie-human and were trying to catch you for some experiment by a Soul Trainer witch named Sybil."

Yori tugged his arm, stopping him. "I didn't know. I thought Jake was trying to kill me."

Dex exhaled. "He may be. The guy is moving up in their ranks, and maybe turning you in or telling them what you were may have given him a boost." He shrugged. "Nash knew what you were before you came out of your cocoon."

She shook her head. "I can't let that stop me from helping you. I can just ask them, and you wait near the cars in case you see him."

"No, I'm not letting you go in there alone." His heart raced. There was always a chance someone might recognize him. Dex hoped the fact that when a person disappeared, people didn't talk about them or search for them worked in his favor.

Dex concentrated on walking casually. "Let's just ask if he is there."

"Okay." She grabbed his hand. Dex flexed his fingers over hers, and they crossed the street.

They made their way up the few steps to the large glass doors of the building. Police officers were either talking to each other or pulling an unwilling person behind them. A few people were just going into the building as though they were there to pick someone up or ask questions.

A lady in front of him went in. Dex grabbed the door as it started to close. There were two ladies at the front desk along with a guy that was a mail attendant who was handing one something.

"C'mon, she looks free." Dex went to the dark-haired girl with almond-shaped eyes who appeared annoyed when he came up to her side of the counter.

"Hey, is Detective Whalen in?" Dex asked in a rush. He didn't realize how nervous he was.

The girl huffed and looked down at the monitor in front of her. After typing a few strokes, she said, "He's booking a suspect."

"I need to talk to him. He told me to meet him here with the stuff he left at—"

"Whatever, I don't care." She grabbed the ringing phone and put her hand up to signal Dex to wait. She covered the phone with her hand. "Go wait for him in his office. It's in the back of the building, in the small blue extension trailer."

"Okay, thanks." Dex exhaled, moving his head to the side to let Yori know it was time to go. He didn't want to be in there any longer than necessary.

They left, but Dex couldn't help glancing at the people

coming and going. He breathed easy since he hadn't recognized anyone.

As busy as it was at the main entrance, the back was pretty quiet. There were only a few police there, a parking lot, and trailers that bordered the lot. The trailers were different colors. The smallest was at the end of the parking lot, set off by itself, and a dingy pastel blue.

"That's his." A patrol car parked in front of it with the number—something he'd never forget since the day the detective arrested him, cuffed his wrist, then shoved him into the car.

A cop coming toward them tossed down a cigarette. "Hey, kid!"

Dex grabbed Yori's hand and walked faster. A thick, tall boy barreled around the other side of the parking lot. He nearly knocked Dex down.

"Get him!" a cop called.

Dex ducked, tugging Yori and dragging her with him to the side door of Detective Whalen's trailer. He pushed the door, and they practically fell into the front room of the compact office.

Yori slammed the door and pressed her back against it while catching her breath. "You almost pulled my arm off! I thought the cop was trying to catch us."

Dex flexed his fists and hopped on the balls of his feet. "Me too." After releasing several breaths, he took two steps back and pivoted. The walls of the office were dingy but covered with pictures of teenaged girls and boys. Black markers littered the table in front of the side wall where a map hung; a red mark traced a jagged line across the surface. Sticky notes were on the faces of the kids on the wall, "found in pieces", "body part found", "clothing or jewelry only" ...and so on. Dex swallowed, remembering the video sent to him by the girl Megan. His girlfriend had been devoured by vampires. Dex had a flash of Grady's severed finger and half-eaten face. He couldn't take in enough air, he had to turn away from the wall.

"I knew some of them," Yori whispered. "My God, that's Cara, she was Megan's best friend. I think Cara even said they were related."

Dex found a chair, sat, and twisted it to watch Yori who touched the freckled-faced brown-haired girl making a funny face at the camera. The picture looked like a year-book photo.

"When I met him, he said they were looking for some serial killer. They had set up a curfew."

Yori snorted and crossed her arms. "There is always someone dying here in the Void."

Dex didn't bother arguing against the truth. He hoped Detective Whalen had answers. He was willing to share what he knew. If the detective did.

·32·

The doorknob rattled. Dex stood up, and Yori fell back into the chair, sliding it behind him.

"I told you, don't send people to my office!" Detective Whalen opened the door, and his eyes searched around the room. His dark hair was sprinkled with gray at the sides. He looked like he'd aged years since Dex last saw him. His hand lay on his holster, and the other held a cellphone. "I'll be damned." He ended the call and moved his hand off his gun.

Detective Whalen narrowed his eyes. "That you Dexter... Dexter Lewis?"

"Hi. Detective."

"You're alive?"

Dex walked up to him. "Where's your son, Kayson?" Last year, the detective seemed taller, thicker than he was. Now, Dex looked down a few inches at him.

"My son? Before I tell you that, I need to know how you survived the crash." The detective walked past him and pointed to the top corner of the back wall. "Not one of your bodies was recovered from the river."

"That's not true. I hit my head when I went under, but I woke up in the hospital, the one near my father's gym."

"That hospital was officially closed to the public a year ago." The detective rushed to his desk drawer. "Come home with me. It's not safe for you here." He frowned then jumped a bit when he noticed Yori, who got up from the chair.

"She's a friend of mine, and can add to what I'm about to tell you." Dex stepped in front of the detective as he started again for the door.

"Fine. Bring her too. You both look like you escaped from jail." The detective waved at them and led them to a small door on the side of the trailer. "Smell like it too."

Dex walked down the few wood-plank stairs of the trailer.

The detective pointed to his vehicle. The black truck had boxes in the cab.

"Climb in the backseat and keep your heads down low. I don't trust these other cops. Lots has changed since your family went missing."

Dex opened the back door and helped Yori get in. The truck was parked on the grass, and no one was around. The field led to a dark alley with dilapidated buildings bordering it. He squinted his eyes; he could swear the buildings seemed to be an illusion. They looked old, but something felt off about them.

"Come on Dex," Yori called.

Dex shook himself out of his daze and climbed in the backseat with her. She moved over to make space for him behind her and laid down. Dex slid behind her and held her in his arms.

The detective started the truck and skidded out of the grass to head down the alley. "Okay, I didn't want to tell you in the office. You never know who is listening. My son is in hiding—out of here. An informant of mine owed me a favor, and I needed to pay it. They were trying to kill my kid."

"Who?"

"The same group that is after your father. We got too

close. Now everyone is pissed about it. Only thing is, they don't really know I'm involved. Your father took the hit for me. The bastard. I told him not to do it."

"Do what? Tell me what's happened."

"In time, in good time. Tell me, you were in the hospital?"

"It's a blur, the ambulance wasn't real, I guess. At the hospital is where they got me. They took me to an underground dungeon. The elite, they are called Soul Thieves. They are powerful, super-human powerful."

"Oh, I know. I saw one at work. Scared the shit out of me. I thought he was a good kid."

"Jake, he is the lead elite at the high school at my school. He also killed London."

"Damnit! He's the kid I was talking about. I saw him choke out my informant, Rocky. He threatened to take the man's kid if he didn't give up information he had on this group that the Overlord is afraid of."

"A group?"

The detective checked the rear mirror as if making sure no one was following them. "The Vigilant. No one knows who they are or how many. They gather information from a powerful informant. They reside here and everywhere. Also, they have the power to go through the in-between. That's something the Soul Warriors try to control and have some type of payment barter system for those they take through. Messy business." He re-adjusted the mirror. "Jake...he's untouchable. I can start trouble for him though—legal trouble."

"He will get away with it." Yori sat up. "He is evil and will do anything to make it from a Soul Thief to become a protégé for one of the twelve."

"Wait? I am not understanding all of this. The twelve,

the elite, Soul Warriors, and the Vigilant... How does that have anything to do with me finding my family and getting out of here?" Dex rested his back against the small door.

"They have everything to do with you getting out of here —or not." A heaviness inflected Detective Whalen's revelation.

Dex didn't like the news. He was starting to think the detective couldn't help him at all.

·33·

"We're here." Detective Whalen cut off the engine.

Dex and Yori sat up.

"Do you have nosey neighbors?" Dex asked.

Detective Whalen's house was the last house on the corner of three-level brownstones. Each was separated by a thin slip of grass and various types of gates. The detective's house was red brick with a thick wooden door and an unmanicured yard that had several feet of weeds wrapped in the wire fence. The weeds leaned over and grew through the pavement leading from the front landing to the front door.

Dex climbed out of the truck. He held Yori at her waist and helped her down.

"Hurry inside." The detective waved them forward as he used a key to unlock the four-foot iron gate.

Dex stepped up the two steps that led to the landing. He pushed the iron gate firmly against the weeds fighting to close it. He waited while Yori secured and locked the gate.

"Are you sure he lives here?" Yori touched Dex's arm.

"I don't know. I never would've thought Kayson's house looked like this. Damn, you can't ever assume you know a person."

The detective opened the door. Expecting them to be close behind he didn't even hold it open for them. Dex jogged up and caught the door before it closed on its own.

He strode into a room near the entry door; it had a small archway. The room held a wood desk and matching file cabinets overflowing with papers. Some papers had fallen onto the floor and were scattered. Dex followed and stood in the doorway. Random bottles of liquor littered the floor. They were all bone empty. Dex glanced at them then back at the detective.

"Come in. There are chairs over there against the wall." Detective Whalen waved a hand while typing on his computer with the other. "Step over the papers. They're research."

"Yeah, if you say so." Dex kicked a bottle out of the way and sat in the chair next to Yori. She seemed to want to help and started to stack some of the papers.

"These are cold cases?" Yori asked. "This one's about the lady who went missing at the library, and her husband went there with a gun demanding they let her out?" She frowned. "He disappeared."

"Him and anyone else who asks too many questions and tries to force an answer." The detective sighed and turned toward them. "First things first, my name is Keith Whalen. Call me Keith."

"You said my father took a hit for you? What did you mean?" Dex leaned forward in the chair and placed his fore-arms on his knees.

Keith scratched his temple. "I asked him to basically set you up. You were on the football team, and I suspected they were involved in some of the disappearances. I wanted someone to infiltrate. My son—well, he was mine, and I knew he wasn't what they wanted."

"Why not? He was a good athlete. He was also on varsity."

"Well, long story, but his mother made a bargain with

someone who made sure he wouldn't make it to the elite. She didn't want that for him. Too bad she paid for it with her life."

Dex frowned. "So, the people who tried to kill my family and I did it because my father let me play football?"

"No, they tried to kill him because of a stupid move I made."

"What's that got to do with my father?"

"He came to me when you got a ring from one of the Soul Thieves' new recruits. He thought you were dying and asked me for help. I got him in touch with someone. Then, I did something stupid." Keith put his hands on his face and dragged them down. "I sent a message—a threat—to Coach Moreau, their number one recruiter. I told him I had something on him that would blow the news about the 'governor' and his dirty dealings in flesh out of the water."

"What dealings?"

"Our governor is a figurehead. Fake and under the control of the twelve. The fake president is another mirage. They are figureheads. Each is a puppet, and those who hide behind them to rule are determined to destroy the people here and from my home. Coach Moreau and he are 'brothers,' and I just...well, I wanted to let him know I was coming after him."

"What did my family have to do with it?"

"Coach Moreau was the one who invited your dad here to open the gym to train his star athletes and those of other 'elite' coaches."

"So, he knew my father had something to do with your threat?"

"Not initially, but he paid your father a visit, and your father—he was pissed because you were hurt. He had gotten in contact with the Vigilant, but he couldn't get you help once the coach was on his back about the threat I made. Your dad almost got away with the trick he played to get the coach off his trail—my trail—but when you returned to school and didn't resume your determination to reach varsity, it made Coach Moreau suspicious. After that, they came after your father."

"Because of me?" Dex balled his fists and narrowed his eyes.

"No, me. Your father was protecting me. He felt what I was doing to bring down the fake governor—all part of 'the twelve' and the kingpin that puppets the president—was too important. I told him to get out, bargained him a way to do it, but they knew you were leaving—really leaving."

"So, it wasn't about my mentor Grady and what the police found in the woods by the club?"

The detective dropped his hands to his sides, his eyes watering. "About Grady, your mentor? I'd been keeping close tabs on you. Your father was reporting to me who your friends were, who came to the gym, who left, and anything that went on around the premises. He told me you got the ring from a friend. I knew the only way that ring would come off was if a Soul Thief died. I'd literally picked up the pieces of what was left of Grady's body two nights before your father practically knocked down my front door, asking me to help save your life—your soul."

"What did you want with that information? There is no justice here for us humans, Detective." Yori dropped the papers she held.

"Revenge. My wife died at the hands of the man at the top. I needed to know who he was. He is a chameleon, a shifter that can change into *any* animal—even a person. That's not typical. I wasn't privy to the magicals that inhabit this place until I started having cases upon cases of deaths that my boss kept telling me to file away into the cold case files. I got sick of it. I dug deeper, not realizing the more I did, the more it revealed about my wife—her ties to this place—and why she brought us here."

"I need to find my brother and sister who are still here. If my parents left..."

"Your mother didn't get out of here. I could only get your father and sister out since they were the only ones healthy enough to go. My son was able to escape also as part of a deal with the contact and protection offered to his child for his help. I don't know where any of them are. Besides," He continued, falling back into the thick leather chair behind his desk, "you are not even fit to fight to get them back."

Dex surged up from his chair. "You don't know me or what I am capable of—not at all."

The detective didn't flinch. "I know you aren't ready for them. A shifter with more power and magic than you can ever imagine, an evil that rivals the very core of evil—Satan —but the one of this realm, world, or whatever this Void we have found ourselves in is."

"Help me, tell me where I can get help."

"I'm trying, but the source is hard to find. I may have to risk asking someone for a favor who will likely request a payment that will possibly kill me."

Yori stood and crossed her arms. "I don't understand."

The detective signed and stood. "Look, it's late. I've got some thinking and favors to cash in. I will get you to safety and help you be ready to save the rest of your family. This is a mess I created, and I'm sorry son—real sorry I used you."

Dex snorted. "I bet."

Keith shrugged off the sarcasm. "There's a room behind the bookshelf. Move the bookshelf, push the wall in, then slide it open. It will take you into the room with a stocked refrigerator, a small shower, bed, and loveseat. Cozy place. If something happens in here, you can escape through a door under the bed. I'm going to my bedroom next door. Goodnight. We can plan in the morning before I go to work." He stumbled out of the room as though he carried the weight of the world on his shoulders.

Dex had a headache. He couldn't shake the feeling that even though things were bad before, maybe contacting detective Whalen wouldn't work out the way he'd thought.

·34·

ex finished his shower and rubbed his thick, curly hair vigorously with one of the two towels he found hanging on the door. He dropped it on the bed and sat on the edge, listening to the soft lilting voice of Yori singing during her bath. The tub had been too small for him to take a bath, but Yori's petite frame fit in it perfectly. He heard the pelting of the shower and figured she'd showered first then decided to take a bath afterward.

The room was warm with soft blue walls, pictures of the beach, and a faux window leading to a pathway into the woods. The loveseat was up against the full-sized bed in the corner of the room. There were no windows, but a skylight on the upward sweep of the ceiling let in the cool night air. It smelled a bit musty with a faint scent of mothballs as if it hadn't been used in a while, and Dex wondered why the room was even there.

He got up and went to the dresser in the corner. It held unisex gym shorts with elastic, large shirts, socks, stretch pajamas, and thin robes. On top of the dresser was a box. Dex opened it and found a brush, comb, conditioner, and aloe water spray. He sprayed a generous portion in his hair with the conditioner and brushed it back from his forehead. He dug a little further and found some hair bands and bushed his hair back into what Yori had called a 'man-bun'. It was good to be clean—really clean, and be able to relax.

Dex felt like the hairs on his body had been standing at attention for longer than he could remember.

He was tired, but he wouldn't fall asleep until Yori came out of the bathroom. She'd become much more than a girl-friend to him. He was literally ill at the thought that she was out of his sight. Dex wanted to protect her, keep her happy, and give her the 'normal' she was looking for as long as he would forever be a part of her life. Problem was, he didn't think normal existed anymore.

Dex grabbed a large shirt and one of the smaller pair of shorts along with the comb and brush before going to the bathroom door. He knocked softly. "Can I put these clothes and comb in there for you?"

Yori's singing stopped. "Clothes? Yes! I'm still in the tub though."

Dex hesitated and said, "I won't come in...if you don't want." He couldn't help but tease her when he'd seen her nearly nude, but he'd always turned away to keep some distance between them.

Yori's response was soft, a bit unsure. "I'm covered in bubbles. It's okay."

Dex opened the door then stopped. There were suds on the floor, the mirror, and the wall.

"I got carried away with the bubble bath. Don't slip."

Dex chuckled and averted his gaze. He placed the clothes on the sink. "It smells good in here."

"That's good, I want to wash months of grime and stink off me. It hurts a girl's feelings when someone says you smell."

"The detective meant that for me, you know." Dex leaned against the wall, his back facing Yori.

"I may fall asleep in here, the water is so soft, warm, the

perfect temperature. I don't even feel magical. No wings, no fear, I feel normal again."

Dex pursed his lips and nodded. "I'm glad you do."

"Ah, I sense some 'brooding' going on."

Soft foam of bubbles hit the side of his neck. By reflex, he turned around. Yori sank deeper into the suds, her chin, face, and hair were packed with bubbles.

Dex laughed. "You are drowning in bubbles!" He belted out another chuckle and bent over to hit his knee. "Priceless. I can't stop."

Yori tossed ball after ball of bubbles at him.

Dex swatted them away while laughing and holding his stomach. "No judgment...seriously."

"Liar."

"I'm leaving now before I get soaked." Dex grabbed the door and ducked just as another bubble-ball flew over his head.

Dex closed the door and leaned against it. Damn, she was beautiful. Her skin, like toffee, peeking out of pink bubbles, made his heart stop; she was adorable. He let his gaze sweep over the room. It landed on a radio with a CD player. Taking several calming deep breaths, he walked over to it and switched it on, turning to a jazz channel. His father always made him work out to it to get his mind centered—whatever that meant. It usually put him to sleep. Now he needed something to calm him before he ruined things with Yori by obsessing over the fact that she'd been nude under the water.

He grabbed one of the sci-fi books from the small bookshelf nightstand on the side of the loveseat. Dex propped his bare feet on the bed and opened the book. Hopefully, the story inside was worse than the one he was living. Maybe it would make the coming days easier.

·35·

The bathroom door creaked open. Dex raised his head, holding his breath for a moment as Yori walked into the room. He smiled at her booty bump that closed the bathroom door.

"You can have the bed if you want. Do you care if my feet use it as a footrest?" He smiled, making light of the fact that inside he was begging her to ask if he could lay on the bed and hold her. His fingers squeezed the edges of the book he'd been holding while he anticipated her response.

Yori frowned. "You don't want to share the bed with me?" Her shoulders dropped.

Dex observed her. The shorts fit her small waist, falling just below the curve of her hips. The t-shirt fit loosely over her stomach. It was the most clothes he'd seen her in since he met her, and yet, it made her even more alluring.

He swallowed. "What do you want? I'd love to sleep next to you and hold you through the night to stop my bad dreams, but I don't want to make any assumptions. You know what they say about assumptions, right?"

She smiled. "Yes, ass-sumptions." Yori walked over to the bed. She climbed on it and crawled to the space against the wall.

Dex waited while she pulled the covers back and slid her feet inside.

Yori patted the pillow next to hers. "Here's a good spot

for you." She kicked her feet under the cover. "I warmed it up for you."

He tossed the book to the floor. Dex climbed in bed with her. Yori snuggled up to his side and intertwined her legs within his.

"One day we won't be able to do this—when we go back to school, our lives..." Yori sighed.

Dex dipped an eyebrow at the dampness he felt on his chest. He hoped she wasn't crying.

"I'll always sleep next to you—if you want me to." His voice came out in a hoarse whisper.

"I want you to, but how would you do it?"

"I'd climb through your window like Romeo did." Dex laughed. "Or draw you a sign on the nearest tree to let you know secretly to leave the window open for me."

"You promise?"

"I do." Dex kissed the top of her head. "You know what else I promise?"

"What?"

"To love you for the rest of my life."

Yori stayed silent. Dex's heart thumped in his chest, and he tightened his hold on her.

"I will love you for the rest of mine, too."

"I will convince my parents to let you live with us— when this is all over."

Yori smiled at him. "You are very convincing." She moved up and kissed him.

Dex closed his eyes and allowed her to lead the kiss. When he couldn't resist the temptation any longer, he twisted and pushed her beneath him as he delved within her sweet mouth. He could kiss her forever. It wasn't the time to take things further. Yori gave him a soft push, so he reluctantly pulled away.

Yori frowned. "Would you be mad if I told you I wasn't ready to take things further? I know you and London must have...and, well, Jake and I did, but..."

Dex put a finger to her mouth. "You are worth waiting for. What I have with you feels deeper and makes me so sated that making love to you will be just the treat I will savor, to enjoy when you know I am worthy."

Her hand rested on his jaw. "Oh. Dex, you are so worthy. I'm the one who has to allow myself to grow enough to trust my judgment. I don't feel strong enough for myself. I love you, but I don't want to be the co-dependent person I was with Jake. I need to find my own strength and my own way so when I give myself to you—it's when I feel worthy."

"You are strong. I know because you risked yourself to stay and make sure I was okay. I have two fierce sisters, and I trust them with my life more than some guys I know. There is strength in what some people may consider weakness— you are strong. The way you show it is different from the way I do. That makes us a good team."

She smiled. "We are a good team, but I need to know that I am able to do this alone when I need to."

"Didn't I tell you I would never leave you alone? Even if we aren't together, you will always be with me." Dex took her hand and placed it to his heart. "Right here."

Yori lifted her head to kiss his chest just above his hand. "Oh, Dex, I do love you so much."

Dex shifted as she turned. He spooned her, kissing the curve of her neck. "I'm starting to think I need a bigger word than love to describe how I feel about you, Yori." He squeezed her a bit tighter, spooning her with his body. The dread over the possibility of being separated from her sat like a cold rock in the pit of his stomach. Dex held her while she nuzzled her lips at the base of his neck to kiss him. He

couldn't let them ever be separated. He had to protect her
—forever.

·36·

They decided to investigate detective Whalen's house. Dex was tired of being cooped up in the room. They ate the breakfast that Keith left them inside the room. Neither of them woke when he entered. Dex didn't realize they'd been so exhausted.

Dex leaned back in the large chair in the detective's home office while Yori sifted through the papers on the floor.

"The man should clean this place." Dex held up a file with no label on it and tossed it on the desk.

"He's obsessed with finding where this guy, the Overlord, lives." Yori stood and placed an aged leather-bound book on the desk. "See here, it's a map of parts of the dark woods. It shows some entrance with a two-headed horse statue."

Dex sat up in the chair. "What does it mean?"

"He had a note here that he thinks it's some type of hidden entrance to an underground city."

Dex shook his head. "I hope that's not where we escaped from."

"I don't know." She sighed and leaned against the desk.

Dex smiled at the checkered sweatpants she wore that were slightly too big. The strings from the waist tie hung down to her knees.

"We can ask him more when he returns. Let's go upstairs, and when we are finished up there, we can search the basement." Dex got out of the chair and followed Yori from the room.

They stopped at the window in the living room across from the office and slid aside the curtains. It was cloudy outside with a slight wind pushing the trees in the yard. No one was walking on the sidewalk or even parked on the street. It was strange, but Dex assumed people were working or kids were in school.

Yori's hand rested on Dex's back. "Ready to go upstairs?"

"Yeah." Dex wondered if the detective had neighbors. He didn't understand how a street could be so dead during the day.

Dex went first up the shiny wood stairs. Tennis shoes lay on one stair and a tossed football practice jersey from their school on another. He got to the top of the stairs, flicking on the light in the hallway with three doors. One was ajar, so Dex walked to that one first.

"A music studio." He pushed it open further and was impressed by some of the posters of Jimi Hendrix and other guitarists on the walls. Padding on each wall was likely to keep down the noise from playing the instruments. Several guitars stood on stands in the corner. Dex picked up a picture of Kayson and Silas with others in their band.

"Wow! He was the guitarist for Dark Knights?" Yori squealed, jumping up and down. She snatched the picture from Dex.

"Dark Knights?" Dex thinned his lips. He didn't like how excited she was about the band. Their lead was a murderer. "You knew about them?"

"Yeah, their debut was the night Grady was killed. They were touring other cities and would do surprise performances, but they wore masks—until they performed at Club Fixation."

"Ah, remember I told you Grady was supposed to take the spot for their keyboardist? Then, he and Silas got into a big argument about it. You laughed when I told you Silas Bane turned demon Fenrir Wolf with fire in his eyes and basically ate Grady." Silas was unhinged, and something must have stopped the guy from chewing Dex up with Grady that night they met.

"If Kayson was in the band and was best friends with Silas, do you think he knew what Silas was...uh, his magical self?"

Dex remembered the roar that sounded in the room where he'd left his sister, EmVee, with Kayson. Could Kayson be like Silas? Dex expelled a long stream of air he'd been holding.

Yori shrugged. "I would guess so. They'd been friends for a long time. The band was super-secret, but no one in it seemed magical. Also, none of them was recruited for the Soul Warriors."

Dex shook his head. "Does anyone ever seem like they are magical? Do you think if Kayson was like Silas—that his father knew? If you met Nash on the street, would you think he was just a regular kid?"

Yori raised an eyebrow. "Nash didn't look normal; he was too attractive with predator eyes that seemed just a touch crazed. I wouldn't have wanted to meet him on the street."

"Let's see what's in the other rooms." Dex grasped the picture of the band from Yori and put it back on the shelf. He gave her a smile. "I'm jealous, okay."

Yori laughed. "Well, they are gorgeous. But they aren't you, who is extremely gorgeous."

Dex smirked. "I'm glad you think so." He grasped her hand, leading her to the next room. Twisting the knob, he opened the door. It smelled like the place had been closed for a while. It was musky and dust was visible in the air from the sun beaming through the window that had a film of dirt on it. It had a full-sized bed, a mural of Kayson throwing the football in a Baltimore Ravens uniform.

"He liked the Ravens? He wanted to go pro-football too?" Dex pointed at the wall. "That must be his dream team to play on."

"Nice team, nice room."

The comforters and rugs were purple, gold, and white—to match Kayson's favorite football team, Dex guessed. He didn't feel comfortable invading the room, but Yori pushed him through the doorway.

Dex walked over to the small desk in the corner. A mess of papers with music notes written on them had been tossed at the base of the lamp. He turned on the lamp and traced the sheets there.

"He played the keyboard too." Yori pulled a portable keyboard from under the bed. It had more sheets of music on top of it.

"My sister didn't say anything about Kayson. She only talked about Silas."

Yori tapped several of the keys, making a nice melody. "I heard she was dating Silas, but Kayson had a thing for her first."

"Well, I didn't like Silas. Kayson, I only trusted him because I had to."

"What—you played football with him? I thought he was on varsity and you were on JV?"

"No, not that. He was in the room with my sister the day in the hospital after our accident. I asked him to get her out of there. I heard a roar—like I had heard with Silas, then a crash. I hope they'd got out of the hospital room, but the window had to be several floors up. Also, an explosion shook the place, and...the rest puts me where I am today."

"I think he was a good guy. He was always nice to me."

"Lewis! And that girl. Come down here." Detective Whalen's voice rang through a speaker on the wall.

Dex dropped the sheet music he was holding. "Guess he knows we were snooping around." He shrugged and waited for Yori to push the keyboard set under the bed.

"There are cameras in here, you know." Yori pointed to the one just outside the room.

"I guess I ignored them."

Yori grasped his hand. "He's a cop. He was trained to be careful and suspicious."

They held hands until Dex stepped onto the first step. He jogged down the stairs with Yori's soft footsteps behind him. Detective Whalen stood in front of his office, the archway surrounding him like the entrance to a fortress.

"Find anything of interest?"

"Yeah, your son and Silas Bane. They were best friends?"

"You can say that."

"Did you know Silas was like a werewolf?"

The detective's eyes dipped down to Dex's feet and back up again. "You know something?"

Dex crossed his arms. "Don't play games with me. Was Kayson also a wolf shifter? While we were prisoners, we met someone named Nash. He knew what Silas Bane was—a killer. A mix of Fenrir Wolf and Soul Trainer. Some kind of experiment that the Soul Warriors are doing to build some crazy hybrid army for something. If my sister is with your son—who was the last person I entrusted her to—I need to know if he is a killer like Silas was. Will he eat my sister? Will she have survived with him like you claimed?"

The detective searched around the room as if making

sure no one else was around. He waved them into the office and turned to lead them in. He collapsed in the chair.

Dex sat in one chair and Yori in the other.

The detective leaned back in his padded chair. It was beginning. The clash with the truth.

·37·

Dex fisted his hands on his knees. "Keith, did your son have the same problem as Silas?"

Detective Whalen sighed. "Were you in the basement?"

"Why? I just need the truth. You knew what Silas was, right? A Fenrir Wolf and Soul Trainer mixed up by someone in a lab. I need to know what your son, his best friend, was." Dex leaned forward. "I sent my sister with him."

"I knew what happened with Silas Bane. The Soul Warriors couldn't control him. He went rogue because one of their own gave him the freedom to kill—their own. They protected him and, well, were afraid of him."

"What-about-your-son?" Dex demanded.

"Silas, he got to him. They were friends. Silas was a charmer for sure. He visited all the time. Then they had a fight. I didn't see the kid for a week or so, and—" the detective mumbled a curse—"Kayson, he transformed into a wolf one night. He'd been out all night. He was going to talk to Silas about their band. Kayson didn't know I had a tracker in his cellphone. I was worried, went to find him and..."

"Did he kill?" Dex swallowed. The thought of his sister being eaten alive like Grady had been made his stomach churn.

The detective released a cry. "He...did, but the person, he was a known suspect. He tried to lock himself in the closed cells I had put you in to keep you hidden from the other police and prisoners. Someone placed a known murderer in there, either to prepare to transport him or to smuggle him out. That's what they do sometimes when a criminal is a magical that they either want to keep hidden or use in some way. My boy tried to do the right thing but ended up killing the prisoner. I got there in time to..."

Dex fisted his hands. "You covered up your son's murder? It doesn't matter if the person he ate was evil; he was worse. Was this before or after you put me in that cell?"

"After, much after. He'd learned to control it, suppress his emotions. Kayson, well, he hadn't turned in a long time. They aren't like werewolves since they aren't controlled by the sun. Kayson could control changes— except when hunger, intense anger, or fear took over. The basement is where he went when he felt the need to...change."

"How the hell would you know if he changed or not?" Dex surged up and screamed, "I sent my sister with a killer?" Dex blinked away tears of frustration. "Why should I trust you now? Why!" He was shaking with restraint. He didn't want the detective to know what he was capable of, not yet.

"Because I want to do what's right for you and your father. I promise you I will have the name of a Vigilant who can help you find and infiltrate the holdings where your siblings were taken. I made contact with someone who has answers."

"How do we know that person can be trusted?"

The detective shrugged. "You don't. You have to take a risk and trust the sources you have."

A succession of soft knocks sounded on the door.

"My contact is here. Go to your room. There's a camera system in there. You can see and hear us, take notes and

174

cues that can help. Hopefully, my contact will give me the information straight."

"Fine." Dex waved to Yori. "We're out."

---

*D*ex sat on the loveseat with Yori next to him as he played with the remote to turn to the house surveillance system. The detective paced slowly before he finally answered the door.

"Come in," the detective gruffly directed as he opened the door wider.

A slight figure entered wearing a black coat and wide hood that hung low, keeping the face in shadow. A scarf was wrapped around the person's neck and covered their lower jaw. Detective Whalen went around his desk. Gloved hands adjusted the scarf and followed the detective into his office.

"Have a seat."

The figure remained at the front of his desk, then removed the hood of the wool coat. Orange curls spilled over the flattened hood.

Yori gasped. She covered her mouth, her muffled cry named the girl. "Megan!"

Dex leaned closer.

Megan's hands were steady as she unraveled the scarf. "I won't be staying long, Keith."

Dex frowned. "She is different with him. She acts older."

"Hum, she could be older. Age is kind of strange here. Some kids do a redo of high school for years but never seem to age."

Dex considered Yori's words, and he had a feeling that was the case with Megan. That she was older, much older than she let on.

The detective straightened his shoulders. "Okay. I need information regarding the contact for the Vigilant I messaged you about."

"I have done so much for you already." Megan's eyes glowed. "I am wondering if the information I shared with you about Silas Bane, and how I could take care of the problem he posed for this town, was worth the soul-stone you retrieved from the body of my dear friend."

"That's the past. I gave you the stone. That's what you asked for in order to make Silas Bane disappear, saving my son from becoming a slave to that demented monster."

"True. Now. What is it you need from me?" Megan leaned closer. "And remember...everything comes with a price."

The detective sighed. His shoulders slouched a bit. "Fine. I'll pay it. I need the location of the Vigilant that can hide a prospect."

Megan's eyes glowed, and she licked her lips. "Oh, Detective, that will come with a grave cost, to you and the one who seeks him."

"What do you mean?" Detective Whalen rested his hands on his hips.

"I mean, I can't give you the location per se, but the person has to retrieve a valuable asset 'to the cause' and give it up for passage to safety. That passage, if they are worthy, will take them to the Vigilant. One treasure will reveal the guardian, and the guardian will verify whether the person is worthy of passage."

"Okay, can you tell me where it is?" The detective wiped a hand down his face.

"Of course, if that is what you want? I will text you a riddle; it will be easy. Then..."

"Spill it. What do you want me to give you this time?"

"I'm sorry, Detective, but it's not that simple. I have gotten myself in a spot of trouble." Megan folded her arms and tapped her chin. "If you were to take the blame for Silas' disappearance—if asked of course, *only if you have no possible choice but to answer with your life*—then I will release this information to you. Only to the pager I gave you and only after the threat revealing my news-source has been diverted. Since my underground *news for favor service* is being blamed for leaking a small piece of information regarding Silas Bane. Accused Silas of being a Fenrir Wolf-god hybrid. One that devoured virgins who happen to be Soul Trainers. If my name has been absolved from any further inspection by those who seek to uncover my methods—my secrets—you will live."

Dex's jaw dropped. Yori covered her mouth with both hands. Dex wanted to yell at the detective to not give in to what Megan requested.

Instead, the detective gave a nod. "As you wish."

·38·

Dex and Yori searched through the books on the shelf in the dust-covered library in the back of the house.

Detective Whalen was finishing a call up in the office.

"I don't see any books with maps in them or hidden maps." Dex tossed another book on the nearby table.

"These are some ancient texts, though. Some are even translated onto these sticky notes and this parchment. I wonder if that was something the detective's wife did." Yori held up a thick piece of parchment paper filled with messages in a fancy cursive script.

Dex wondered why she would use parchment paper for it. "She could have just used a notebook."

Yori shrugged. "Maybe there is a reason she didn't."

"There was." Detective Whalen stepped into the library. "She liked writing on parchment paper; she thought it was soothing."

"We have no idea what we are looking for. You have any clues yet?" Dex leaned on the shelf and crossed his legs.

The detective wore jeans and a t-shirt. It made him look younger, less serious. "She fed me the first clue. It was with a warning that someone will be here in a few days to ask questions."

"You do know she basically told you that you could die?" Dex curled his lips, disgusted at what Megan had demanded.

179

"Not quite. There is a way out of the dying part. That's the worst-case scenario. Megan always allows for ways to escape. Part of the riddle for me is finding them. The way out that gets me the information you need and saves my life in the process."

"What's the first part of the riddle?" Yori asked. "We can search for a map that has it."

The detective sighed. "Here it goes, I've never been good at these. *A cloud was my mother, the wind is my father, my son is the cool stream, and my daughter is the fruit of the land. A rainbow is my bed, the earth my final resting place. What am I?* I wish I knew."

Dex was at a loss with riddles. They were never his thing. But he could guess. "What comes from clouds, wind, and makes something?"

Yori walked over. "What causes a rainbow?" She jumped up and down, "Rain! Rain!"

"Sounds right to me," the detective confirmed. "So we have to find a place here, or near here, that always rains."

"I did see a map...hmmm." Yori pursed her lips and tapped with her forefinger.

Dex smiled. He studied Yori's face while she was in deep thought. Thing was, he really wanted to kiss her but shrugged it away. "Do you remember a map from when your father and you were together?"

Her eyes brightened. "Yes, that's it. There is a rainy part of the Darkwood Forest that borders the Hound Guard Briars."

Detective Whalen frowned. "Those aren't on any of the maps of this state. Rhode Island doesn't have those on Google maps."

"Nope. Yori's father had ancient maps." Dex turned to her.

"Yes, he did. What we have on the internet or phone apps will not have these locations on them. How could Megan give you a location that you wouldn't even be able to find?" Yori asked.

"I don't understand her methods. I hope she sends me coordinates."

Dex snorted. "Not likely."

Yori bit her lower lip. "Megan, she knows things. Since she knew you were at risk of not surviving your payment for her information, do you think she intended the message for someone else?"

The detective nodded. "Likely. The girl isn't normal. I don't know what she is. Hell, I don't even know if her real name is Megan. Everything I researched on her comes up with blanks."

"Can we trust her?" Dex folded his arms and rocked on his heels. He had doubts, but they didn't have any other options.

"Yes." The detective handed Dex a pager. "Here is the device. It begins. I am giving this to you since it's a sign that whatever she set me up with is coming soon."

Dex took the pager. It was black with an analog screen. A green message scrolled across with a slight vibration. *Whoever holds this, know that Keith Whalen paid a hefty price for your passage. Repay it by serving the teacher you seek—and well. Know there will be a price for you to pay also. Be willing.* Dex almost dropped it.

"What's wrong?" Yori held out her hand as if to take the pager from him.

Dex stuffed it in his back pocket. "Nothing. I don't think I've ever seen a pager this old up close."

"The map you are looking for is likely hidden. She kept the special ones out of sight." The detective went to the corner adjacent to the window, lifted a small file cabinet off the paisley decorated rug, and set it down. He lifted the rug, kicked on a floorboard several times before crouching. He reached in his pocket and pulled out a pocketknife, flicked it open, and used it to pry up the floorboard. The detective removed the floorboard and dug inside of the hidden space. "Here. These three maps she created, and...well, some of her talents were for discovery. Where I am a detective of what I perceive as humans, she was a detective for magicals."

"How long have you known about her...abilities?" Yori picked up the maps he tossed on the floor. She sat crossed legged and opened one.

"Not long before she disappeared. She kept it from me. I thought she was a housewife taking care of our baby, cooking dinner, and cleaning. She was solving mysteries I didn't know existed until clues showed up on my desk from anonymous tips—I didn't know it was my own wife giving them to me."

Dex looked over her shoulder. "It's not written in English."

The detective chuckled. "It is. You just have to know how to decipher it." He pulled a lighter out of his pocket, moving the flame close to the parchment. "She mentioned fire would reveal her secrets. I never considered what it meant until I investigated what she did in this library."

As the flame touched the parchment, cryptic symbols revealed words that explained and detailed the names of places on the map.

Dex gulped at the first message: *The hidden world in my hell called the Void.*

·39·

Someone banged on the front door. Their knocking shook the windows on the lower level. The sound echoed upstairs. Dex grabbed the maps and gathered them in his arms. They ran down the steps and scrambled into the office.

Detective Whalen checked his gun. "I was hoping it wouldn't come to this." He put it back in its holster. "I should've known she wouldn't give us much time!" Detective Whalen cursed and threw the papers on his desk to the floor. "Hide, and be prepared to leave. Take the maps! Now. Get what information you can. If possible, warn the Vigilant."

"Are you going to open the door?" Yori squeezed her fingers with her other hand.

"No, I'll let them bust in. It'll give you more time. Now go!"

Dex grabbed Yori's hand and they entered the hidden room just as someone splintered through the front door. He scrambled to the couch, grabbing the remote that revealed the multiple cameras within the house. Soul Thieves poured into the front hall.

Their dark clothing was similar in style and cut but different depending on either their rank or size, Dex guessed. They stormed up the stairs, into the rooms, tossing things around as if looking for something. The men were angry and determined to find—something or someone.

"They have guns," Yori whispered and pointed at the guy standing in front of Detective Whalen.

"I know him. Coach Moreau, the varsity football coach from school." Dex's fists tightened.

"Turn up the volume." Yori placed a hand over Dex's.

"Wait, there are earphones." Dex scrambled one hand in the drawer on the table, his eyes never leaving the screen. He put one earpiece of the headphones up to his ear.

"The necklace! Where is it?" Coach Moreau slammed a hand on the desk, shattering the middle then kicking the largest piece as it fell apart.

The detective barely flinched. He shrugged. "What are you talking about, Moreau?"

"Don't play stupid with me! The mortician spilled information referring to you as the last person to see that body before it was taken to the morgue. She was one of ours! The necklace around her neck wouldn't have come off unless it was cut off her dead body." He pointed. "Your name is on the crime scene report, that one, and all of the others from the so-called serial killer. She and one other were the only two missing their soul-stones."

"I don't know what a soul-stone is. Why would I remove evidence when I am trying to find the killer too?" Detective Whalen placed his hands on his hips.

"Don't bullshit me! Your son went missing—conveniently—and his best friend did too, shortly after the necklace disappeared. There was a ring from a boy—a Soul Thief in training who also went missing."

Detective Whalen frowned. "I need names to help you, Moreau. If I share all I know, will you leave?"

Coach Moreau smiled. "Depends."

"I don't know anything about what this jewelry does, so I can't investigate who would need it."

The coach narrowed his eyes. "It's magic, powerful, and whoever touches it that isn't properly initiated and of the lineage, will die. So, if you have it in your possession and you are still alive, then you haven't put it on your body or touched the stone."

"Mr. Moreau, I don't have the items you seek. I am investigating these murders, and sadly, we haven't had any witnesses or leads on the valuable pieces you mentioned. If you can tell me more about the victims, I may be able to help."

"Tell me what you know."

"The boy, Grady, both he and his sister were found murdered. They were the most recent victims of the supposed serial killer. The boy was in pieces; his sister London—sucked dry of all blood. Her head was severed. No necklace was found on her body."

Coach Moreau's eyes narrowed. "We have London's necklace, returned by one of our own. He said your son had something to do with it, and you may have covered it up."

Dex frowned. Was Jake trying to set up detective Whalen for killing London?

"What victim was missing a necklace?"

"You know her. Cara, the one whose neck and face were mauled." Coach Moreau pushed the detective in the chest, sending him flying into the wall.

Dex growled. "There were more mauled by Silas?"

"What?!" Yori whispered. "She was Megan's friend. You don't think Silas killed her?"

"I don't know. Jake may know more about the murders or who's trying to copycat Silas's murders. Sounds like there are deaths that Jake recovers the stones. But the murders that Silas did on his own, Detective Whalen was able to recover the stones."

"This goes deeper than we thought. Jake killing for his own purpose, maybe trying to gather power on his own? That wouldn't be good."

Dex frowned at the visual from the other parts of the house. "They are setting the place on fire."

"No!" Yori covered her mouth.

"They are going to kill him when they get the information they want."

"We have to do something to help him." Dex dropped the control. "Search the place for weapons. There are too many of them to handle alone."

Yori yelped. "Too late," she whispered. "Moreau broke his neck with one bare hand."

An explosion rocked the house.

"Let's get out of here!" Dex grabbed Yori's hand. He let it go while he pushed the bed out of the way.

"I have to get us some stuff." Yori threw whatever she could grab into a backpack from the floor. "I got the maps and the lighter for fire. Some food, I-I..."

Dex opened the hatch on the floorboard. He extended his hand. "You go first."

Yori nodded, put the backpack on, then dropped down into the underground tunnel.

Dex followed, slowly lowering the bed back into place then letting the hatch close down above him. He released the breath he'd been holding.

"First stop, the forest." Pushing back his shoulder, he nudged the hatch up higher.

Yori waited, letting Dex lead the way. Coach Moreau was higher up in the organization than Dex realized. The man obviously put the hit out on his father and family. Dex wouldn't forget him. Not at all.

·40·

The tunnel leading to the street was clear. The surface of the walls was smooth cement with metal portions that seemed to be for repairs. Small lights in the ceiling were dingy with dust, but with each step, they glowed.

An explosion rocked the tunnel and threw them forward. He hopped up. He helped Yori pull herself to her feet. A thundering clamored behind them. Dex turned to glance behind him, and the tunnel had caved in.

"There's no going back." There was a heaviness in his chest at leaving the one place he'd felt comfortable sleeping in months. He and Yori had to be careful but quick in their navigation of it.

"Look!" Yori pointed at the cracks in the wall that spread above them.

"We need to hurry!" He grasped her arm to pull her with him. "I think this is next to the sewer system tunnels. I smell water, stank water, and dampness."

They ran. The ceiling groaned. Large and small pieces of concrete, and dirt dropped like hailstones all around. The tunnel ended at a metal ladder leading up to the manhole door to the street.

Light from a streetlight or the moon cast a glow over the ladder.

Dex hopped onto the ladder, said, "Stay close," and then hurried upward. He pushed up the lid to the manhole, grunting before forcing it to turn where nails were rusted shut. With a groan, it released, and Dex moved it aside. He inched his head up and peeked out at the alley where it opened.

He hopped out of the hole, taking another quick look around. The street was clear. No cars were coming, and the sidewalk was lit with lamps. Dex squatted to help Yori out. Dex wiped his hands on his jeans.

She pointed. "We should head north to the edge of town to the largest library. Behind it is the entrance to the rainy part of the forest."

Yori rubbed her arms over the long sleeves on her sweat-shirt she'd borrowed from Kayson's room. Dex had put on a pair of the guy's jeans, a long sleeve shirt, and grabbed one of his jackets.

"You cold? Let me hold the backpack while you put on your jacket." Dex helped her take off the backpack.

"Thanks. I forgot to put on my jacket all the way. Running for your life and grabbing the maps..." She shrugged.

"I know." He put the backpack on and wrapped an arm around her. "Let's walk. I think I know where you are talking about. I spent more hours than I realized driving this town, taking deliveries from the gym and pickups for my father."

"It's a long walk." Her shoulders dropped.

"We can make it. I'll carry you if I have to."

"Thanks." Yori sighed and wrapped an arm around his waist. The sounds of their steps were soft on the pavement. Yori's slippers were soft-footed remains from Detective Whalen's wife. Dex had stuffed his feet into Kayson's tennis shoes he wished were a half size larger.

"I can't believe this. Coach Moreau is an evil bastard.

They were looking for the jewels from the dead Soul Warriors?" Dex exhaled.

"They recycle the magic. Kayson's mother kept a diary of what she learned about them. It was amazing what she was able to record."

"Well, the books burned up with everything else in that house. I'm shook at the way Detective Whalen protected us."

"I'll never be able to forget the image of Coach Moreau lifting him up with one hand and snapping his neck." Yori shivered.

"Me neither. We need it to feed us. We will finish this, find the Vigilant contact, locate my parents, and get help in paying back the Soul Warriors for killing good people."

"Revenge." Yori snorted. "Does it ever end? How will we be able to live a normal life here after this?"

"We aren't staying in the Void. My family wanted to leave here—and I vow to do whatever I can to make it happen and take you with us."

"They say some magicals can't pass through to the other side. The evil within them won't allow passage through the princess who's spirit covers the majority of the entrance like a veil. The only way is to deal with a Soul Warrior that wants to profit from their ability to get through the 'in between.' The only way to find those people that I know of are, well, from...Megan."

Dex frowned, pulling her closer as they left the deserted alley to walk on the sidewalk. Brownstones lined the street. The streetlights flickered on. A few people were walking on the opposite side of the street, weaving through the cars littered alongside the sidewalk.

"I will find a way. There is always a way." Dex prayed there was, that he could make freedom happen. The more things that were being revealed to him, the harder it was to hold onto hope.

They walked for a while; the streets were empty, and the coolness of night hung over them with a touch of dampness.

"I'm so tired." Yori yawned.

"Me too, I'll try to find us a place to sleep." Dex searched the main road of the shopping district of town where they'd exited. They were only halfway to the library at the edge of the city. The stores they'd passed had decorative fronts with lights and creative art that differentiated one shop from another.

Dex used his heightened sense of smell to see if there were any other people or things around them. He didn't smell anything weird or off. If there was anyone in their stores or living on top of the shops in apartments, the scents matched. He inhaled a bit deeper as they walked to make sure nothing smelled out of place.

Yori had slowed her steps. She was practically falling asleep on her feet. He gave her a slight shake. Dex clapped his hands. He spotted a U-Haul lot tucked between a bike shop and a gas station. "Hey, I found us a place to sleep. We can get a few hours before daylight."

Yori perked up and stretched while Dex crossed the street to the small rental lot.

"See, here are some open bed trailers we can sleep on." Dex pointed at a line of silver and beat-up trailers in a row on the side of the building.

Yori shook her head. "You said London was killed by vampires, I guess there aren't many of them, but sleeping out in the open might be tempting the possibility."

"Yeah, right. Let me check one of the closed trailers." Dex approached, tried the lock, and opened it. "Yes! This one is open." A tingle of awareness raced up his spine and produced an urgency to hurry. Maybe it was Yori's warning, but he picked her up and pushed her in, following quickly. He closed the hatch softly, listening to the sounds outside. It was quiet.

Dex stayed near the door while Yori got comfortable behind him. He heard her movements but muted them as he concentrated on what, if anything, was happening outside of the trailer. It was quiet.

"We're good." Dex pushed himself across the floor to the corner. "You can use me as your pillow."

Yori giggled. "You're always my pillow."

Dex leaned against the metal wall, hating that he felt like he was back in his cell in the underground world that had opened his eyes to more terror than he thought possible. He mentally shook off the fear and the anxiousness shaking him and hugged Yori close.

It wasn't long before she started to snore softly. She was exhausted. He was too, but he held on to wakefulness, making sure they were alright.

The moment he started to doze off, he heard it. Someone was jumping from one top of a trailer to another. He prayed whoever it was skipped theirs.

Dex held his breath, squeezing Yori just a bit tighter. There were several of them. Dex counted one, then two, three, and four. Each jumper seemed to land harder on top of the trailers—but they went on. He relaxed, but only for a moment before one more jumper, who must have lagged behind, landed on the roof of their trailer.

The scratch of a nail or claw, whatever it was, made Dex tense. He prayed, *God, please let it pass.*

The trailer shook from the creature on top hopping.

It jiggled the handle. Another sharp cry teased Dex's ears. Whatever it was stopped. It clawed its way back to the

191

top. After several growls and a snarl, there was a slow scratch of a claw. A minute or so passed. Heavy breathing teased Dex's ears. The creature took one final jump, causing the trailer to move to its own rhythm, then nothing.

Dex waited for as long as he could before exhaustion brought a forced peace.

·41·

The pager vibrated against his hip. Light from a crack in the trailer wall teased his eyelids. Dex moved his head side to side then sat up. Yori was curled up next to him with her head resting on his arm. He kissed her forehead as he slid his arm from under her neck. The pager vibrated, and he reached into his pocket to pull it out. The glowing of a rolling message repeated itself over and over again. This was a new clue. He guessed something to be added to the original one they'd decoded to mean *rain*.

Within the water, it stands alone, drab, dark, ugly, but within its power brightly shown.

Dex hated these riddles. He'd never liked playing games, and Megan was known for them. How the girl had the time to concoct them, he never knew. It seemed she had some type of sixth sense or something.

Yori stirred.

He stared at the message, hoping his mind would kick in to decipher the clue.

"What are you looking at?" Yori leaned over his hand. "Did she send another message?"

"Stupid message. Why can't she just tell us what we need to know?" Dex snorted.

Yori took the pager from him.

Dex smiled when she bit her lip and narrowed her eyes. She crossed her legs then bent over the pager.

He couldn't deny he was happy that she would come

closer to unraveling it than he did. So, he stretched. Starting into his calming exercise routine, he did a few pushups, sit-ups, more stretching, then planks.

"I got it!" Yori wiggled her neck in a contained victory dance. "A wand or scepter, something that doesn't look like it but that has some type of magical ability."

"Figures. She'll probably want us to deliver it to her in exchange for our lives." Dex stood.

"She doesn't do that. Megan isn't a killer. Not really."

"You mean she doesn't do the killing. Megan sets people up to get killed." Dex smirked.

"Maybe, but it seems like her intentions are in a good place. I'm sure it's for a good reason."

"I don't know. We'll see. I don't want to end up like Detective Whalen. He didn't exactly deserve to be killed."

Yori pulled the backpack into her lap. "Hand sanitizer? Toothpaste?" She took some of the toothpaste out and put it on her finger then rubbed it over her teeth.

"You saying my breath stinks?" He grabbed the tooth-paste, squeezed some on his tongue, then brushed his finger over his teeth like she had done.

"Water?" Yori smiled and handed him a small bottle of water.

Not with words but actions. Dex laughed. He took just a sip; he didn't want to waste it. "Thanks, you take good care of me."

"No, you have taken care of me. I'm alive now, and not some type of meal for Nash."

"To be fair, he promised not to consume you. I think he liked you...but not as much as I do."

"I can't believe I kissed him." Yori smacked her lips. "He was a monster." She shivered.

"Yes, he was, but he saved us, or tried to." Dex grabbed

the backpack and put it on. "And you were hypnotized by his magic when you kissed him, right?" Dex lifted an eyebrow.

"Still, yuck." Yori stood.

Dex opened the door. He was glad whatever creatures were playing around last night didn't bother trying to open any of the storage trailers. That would have made for a long night.

The brightness of daylight caused him to squint, but he didn't mind. His heart sped up with the anticipation of the day. Maybe it was time to test a friendship. He swung the backpack around, and it hit his chest. Dex reached inside and rummaged through the bag's contents to find the small cellphone he didn't use at Detective Whalen's house.

Yori hopped out of the trailer. "I forgot that was in there."

Dex smiled. "Time to call in a favor, a ride, and maybe buy him a meal." He turned it on, waited for the phone to light up, and laughed out loud at the glaring message. *Call me! ~ Milo* :P

·42·

Milo's blue Jeep sped into the U-Haul parking lot and screeched to a stop. Dex opened the back door for Yori then climbed in the front with Milo.

"Thanks for meeting us. It's been a rough few days."

"Weeks, but I'm not mad. I was worried about you— thought you disappeared." Milo started the car. "There's food in the cooler in the back."

"I got it." Yori handed a sandwich to Dex.

"This looks good." Dex took a bite.

Milo hit the gas. The tires screeched. "Did you hear the news?"

Dex kept eating. He grabbed the water Yori handed him.

She poked her head between the seats. "What news?"

"Detective Whalen's house caught on fire. They accused him of turning into a dirty cop and said he killed himself in a fire, trying to destroy the evidence. Apparently, he killed several kids in a copycat murder and even stole some of the remains' personal effects. Sick. Never would have thought him capable of that."

Dex stuffed the rest of the sandwich into his mouth. It tasted like dirt since he was fighting not to throw up. He didn't like the image of the fire and Detective Whalen's death that flashed in his mind. The fact they were setting it up to make him into a villain made Dex sick.

"Don't believe everything you hear. There's always another side to the story."

Milo nodded. "You're right." He shrugged.

"I appreciate you giving us a ride to the old library." Yori patted Milo's shoulder.

"You sure you want to go there? The place is rumored to be haunted and dangerous. It's not even open to the public. The only people I know who could get in there are the fraternity guys from the universities."

"We want to get dropped off there. We aren't going in." Dex wiped the back of his hand across his face.

"My house is on the way. Did you want to stop over? I can let you shower, and I have extra clothes."

"I don't know. That's asking a lot, and I want to get over there before it's dark."

"Suit yourself. It's only a half an hour away."

"Good." Dex brushed off Milo's snarky tone. "What's been up with you? Football practice? Did you make the lacrosse team?"

Milo exhaled and hit the steering wheel. "No, I didn't make it. I'm stuck being a subpar player on a low-level team." He shrugged. "It's alright. I got a backup plan. I've been invited to work for one of the head coaches of the Purview High School team as his gofer. It's a coveted job."

"That's good. I'm happy for you. How'd you get it?"

"I had to submit an essay, resumé, and DNA test."

Dex knew from experience that didn't sound good. "I thought you were a shifter? Did you want them to find that out about you? A DNA test seems dangerous."

Milo smirked. "I didn't send them my DNA."

Laughing, Dex elbowed him. "Smart. Where'd you get fake DNA? I may need some."

"Girl named Megan can get you anything for a price. I need to get into the elite here. I need answers."

Dex wanted to warn him, tell him more, but it was best he didn't. The less Milo knew, the better. "Be careful, Megan's like a death dealer or something. Nothing she does for you comes out the way you would think."

Milo shrugged. "I'm desperate, and she's the only person that I can trust to get me where I want."

"Well, if you get in and find the answers you seek, promise me if you find any information about someone named Rei or Reece, text me, and I will be forever grateful."

"Rei and Reece? Rhyming names. Funny, sounds like twins."

Dex didn't want to tell him too much about his younger twin siblings. He wanted Milo to help them if his deep-dive into parts of the Soul Warrior organization led him across them. "Just remember the names. If you hear anything, text me."

Milo winked. "I got you." He parked in front of the library.

"Thanks for the ride and the food." He held out his hand. "And for being a friend—a real one."

"I hope you believe that. I'm here if you need me."

"And if you need me, I'm keeping the phone, so let me know."

"Good as done."

Dex got out of the car and turned to the library while Yori said her goodbyes. Now, to find rain in the forest and some type of rod within. Dex grasped Yori's hand and walked toward the beaten-down grass path. They got to the broken part of the iron gate leading to Darkwood Forest. Dex didn't feel excited. Instead, exhaustion hit, and he was ready for this journey to be over.

·43·

The thick brush and woods behind the gate had a heaviness to it that Dex hadn't felt before they crossed over. The library seemed completely deserted but felt as if it was watching.

"The library is closed, right?" Yori whispered as she brushed an elbow against Dex's arm.

"Milo said it was, and it would only be open certain times. Let's keep going, though."

Yori handed Dex the backpack. "It's getting heavy. Hopefully it's waterproof."

Dex put on the backpack. "It is. I can tell. I was a backpack connoisseur in the day—when I lived in New York and had to wear one to carry my tagging equipment. Besides, that's the only word I remember from my French class. I spent most of the time in class sketching."

"I guess backpacks would be needed. I didn't like them. I had handbags I designed myself." She frowned.

"I didn't know you did that. I always liked the designs on the bags you wore at school. They got my attention in art class." The trees thickened, and a light cloud hung low. It drizzled beyond the new barrier of trees.

"I'm glad you liked them. A few teachers asked me to make them some. It was profitable for me and kept me fed since my father's disappearance."

Dex pointed at the cloud. "It looks different further in."

A drizzle of rain remained behind the thicker set of trees. "I think we'll lose some sun when we go in."

"I packed a flashlight, but it still isn't night time." Yori tugged on Dex's arm and pulled down the backpack. She rummaged inside and wiggled the flashlight in front of him.

"I don't need it." Dex pushed it back to her. "But you use it."

Yori bit her lower lip. "Why don't you need it?"

"I didn't tell you before because I wasn't sure, but when Izume attacked me with the other leopard shifters, they changed me. I have some of their qualities. I can see in the dark."

"Can you shift? Like into one of them."

"No, she told me that wasn't possible. It was some sort of mating ritual done by accident, so I wouldn't get the same benefits as one of their mates they were marrying. I'd have some heightened qualities but wouldn't be able to shift or use their shifter magic."

"Why didn't you tell me before?" Her voice trembled.

"I didn't want to scare you since I didn't know what it meant."

"I'm hurt. I shared everything with you. I thought you trusted me to do the same."

Dex placed a hand on her shoulder. He didn't want them going further before he set things straight. He swallowed as he turned her around. "Yori. You mean more to me than anyone. I don't want you to feel like I don't trust you. I like to process things myself, in my head, before I share with you. I love you. So much it scares me, and I don't want to ruin us. I want to try to find a sliver of peace in whatever minute I get to spend with you where there is no drama. Finding my family, defining what it means to be a Vigilant, getting answers and help, it's wrecking my mind. I don't want to bring you into that space."

Yori placed her hands on his cheek and stood on her tiptoes. "I'm here with you, Dex. Right here."

"Thanks for forgiving me." He kissed her. Dex lifted her up in his arms for a hug.

Dex secured the backpack, making sure it was tightly closed. He still wanted to keep it intact and on him. The rain fell at a light pace. A mist formed between the trees that made the area appear skewed and blurry. He didn't see rain but assumed it was raining harder there.

Dex crossed the barrier of bushes and dead leaves with Yori close behind him. He came to an abrupt stop; his jaw dropping at the sight. Raindrops had become suspended in mid-air. The mist had thinned, and the forest was green with lush vegetation hugging the trees and lining the ground. The smell was sour, laced with the dampness of the water and something like the stink of fertilizer.

"What...how is this happening?" Yori covered her mouth.

Raindrops were falling on his head, but with one step further, he'd hit the area with the suspended rain. He gulped back the lump in his chest. There were so many things that suspended raindrops could mean about the atmosphere in front of them.

"I don't know. Maybe we just have to take a risk to find out." Dex stepped forward. The suspended drops splashed on him and bounced off. Some splashed, but others bounced off to move slightly away. Some magnetic pull must have been keeping them in place, but Dex didn't know why he didn't feel it. The droplets that burst on his face and hands felt cool to his skin. Despite the suspended drops of rain, the echo of a raging thunderstorm vibrated around them. The ground shook with each clap of thunder. The sky was thick with clouds that trembled with lightning yet to burst.

He measured his steps and pushed his hand forward to move the drops out of the way. Some of them bounced while a few popped, but he couldn't take his eyes off of the phenomena beyond the suspended raindrops.

What looked like a tornado, self-contained by some invisible force, threatened to break the suspended peace of the raindrop forest. For some reason, it never moved forward but loomed ahead like a roaring lion, warning them not to go further.

"This is..."

"Unbelievable." Yori gasped.

·44·

Dex hesitated. "One clue was rain; I think we found that."

"The other was a wand or scepter." Yori cleared her throat. "I'm sure getting to it won't be easy."

"What does the map show?"

"Nothing further in. It pointed past the gate and there were teardrops that now I see were this raindrop part of the forest. That was all."

"Okay." Dex gradually moved them through the suspended rain part of the forest. The clacks of thunder made him stop here and there on the way. It seemed to be getting closer, mostly centered in the anomaly of an enclosed storm. How a storm could stay suspended in such a small area by some type of invisible wall, Dex didn't know. Was it magic? Science? Gravity? He wished he'd paid more attention in science class.

Dex stopped in front of the barrier that separated them from the raging storm. He shrugged. Holding out his hands, he touched the pouring rain. Dex snatched his hands back. "It's cold." Giving Yori a nod, he added, "Stay close." He surged ahead with his shoulder.

Cold and drenching rain enveloped them. It was hard to see except for the occasional breaks in the rhythm of the pounding rain. Every so often, it was as if the clouds needed to take a break, and the rain receded in parts as other clouds pushed it to the other side of the field of grass. The clouds were thick but illuminated with light from lightning bolts that seemed to build up within them. The ground was covered in thick and stringy brown vines from the sporadic trees with dark-tipped branches and no leaves. The thick vines were overrunning the grass. Virtually, a vine-covered dirt path that made it hard to get a sure footing in the rain.

The rain pelted them in waves. Dex searched but didn't see anything odd or protruding from any of the seemingly dead trees. He stepped over several thick vines, glancing back to make sure Yori wasn't too far away. She had stopped to inspect a rock at the foot of one of the barren trees.

Dex blinked. About eye-level, the tree had a hollow opening that looked a lot like a mouth. In a flash, it closed then opened again as it was seeking to drink the rainwater that was drenching them. The movement was so fast, Dex wondered if he'd imagined it. The wind churned around them as if it was a living force of its own, and with it, drew the rain in slanted patterns.

"Wait! You see that tree?" Dex watched the tree, waiting for the hollow opening in it to move again, but nothing happened. So, maybe he had imagined it after all. Like the wind had lured the rain away, they got a break as it lightened. He had to be seeing things. It was raining too hard to be sure. "Be ready for anything. Things aren't what they seem." The tingling of adrenaline rushed through him as if propelled by rocket power.

"I am."

"It's letting up...the rain, it's slowing down," Dex called to Yori.

"I don't think so." She pointed to the wall of rain circling back around to them. "There's just a break in it."

"That sucks." Dex dropped his shoulders; the break was a clue. Only thing was he didn't feel too happy about it. "Let's walk further inward. It looks like the rain only falls on the outer part of this area of the forest. If we go deeper in, it's clear." Dex pointed at the clouds.

Yori narrowed her eyes at the tree next to them. "It moved! The tree. It moved."

"What?" Dex timed the break in the beating rain. "Damn! I thought my eyes were playing tricks on me." Dex grabbed Yori's hand. "Run for the break."

He sprinted at top speed, practically dragging her. He didn't know how to tell her that if they'd stayed longer, he was afraid they wouldn't make it. The rain was heavy when they first passed through the suspended rain forest. Then, the breaks in the pouring rain appeared as they notice trees moving. He had a feeling that everything they did was timed and staying too long in one place was a bad idea.

Yori kept up with him. Dex didn't go at his top speed; he wanted to keep pace with her. The rain pelted them repeatedly then gave them a bit of a break, just to take a deep breath before it pounded them again. The wind mixed with rain made their wet shoes slide in the leaf-littered mud. Dex wondered if there was a time the place ever saw the sun. The thought made him frown.

A break in the curtain of rain provided a moment of light mist in place of the deluge. He burst through the clutter of barren trees. The ground was moss-covered. The rain pounded behind them and to the side, but not within. They faced a waterway, a swamp with brackish water and full green trees that hugged the narrow passage beyond the clearing. The trees were large with their fat branches bursting from the ground with a dusting of green. Some were so well-formed they appeared to have formations of a body or some type of beast climbing its way out from the ground. Vines were fashioned like arms clawing their way from underground, and mud mixed with leaves to form a head facedown.

Yori touched Dex's arm. "This might be it. The place where we can find the scepter."

Dex swallowed. He was sure this was it. Something about the part of the journey made him uncomfortable. There was a smell, sweet yet metallic in the air. Crackling echoed around them.

"The vines!" Yori grasped the sleeve of Dex's jacket. "They're moving."

Dex tugged her close to him. She was frozen, her eyes the only things moving as they jumped from one forming creature to the next. They were shaping at a rapid pace. Dex stepped back. Yori's hand hit his chest as they pivoted to see others growing behind them.

Each of the vines slithered in to form creatures made from bark, moss, dirt, and mud. They pushed themselves out of the ground, creating enormous dipped mounds in the forest that Dex feared just as much as the creatures. Their faces were fashioned of mud and leaves with ominous black emptiness in place of their eyes. Their open mouths seemed cluttered with thorns for teeth. Some appeared to be shaped in ways to mock the human form; others were like trees that sprouted legs and arms.

"I don't think these Tree-folk are friendly." Yori shook her head and took a step back.

"No, they aren't, but neither are we." Dex touched her shoulder. "Don't hold back. I mean it. We both need to survive this."

Yori exhaled, blowing softly. "I won't..."

Dex sensed the blow before it connected. One of the tree-men vines interlaced from his torso into a hammer. Its legs grew with each step the creature took toward him. Its hammered arm hit Dex in the stomach, sending Yori hurling through the air. His back connected with another firm bark he'd hoped was a benign tree. Shaking his head, he searched for Yori. Tight, unforgiving trunks wrapped around his torso.

Yori yelped and fluttered away from others who attacked her with multiple jutting branches. Her wings expanded, and the silver designs on her face extended around her eyes and up her forehead. One tree-folk grabbed her wings and pounded her body to the ground. Yori kicked back. Sprinkles of blue magic expelled from her feet. The tree-man released her wings, and Yori skirted away.

Dex surged toward them, but the branch-made hammer whacked him harder. He shook off the dizziness. With a yell, Dex flexed his arms, butted his head back, and squirmed enough to be set free. He landed on his feet, sliding a bit in the mud. Another thick tree creature with a hollow mouth wrapped its vines around Dex's neck and jerked him forward. Dex kneed it in a weak spot on the side of its head.

Yori screamed. Dex punched the tree-man repeatedly then kicked back at another charging him. Dex ran toward her. She struggled as one tree-woman lifted Yori to its chest. The tree was giant. The vines separated, forming a black void where its stomach should have been. Yori braced her feet on each side of the opening. She jerked side-to-side, struggling to break free of the vines surrounding her upper arms.

Dex lurched toward her. "Fight it!" He was brought up short as one of them grabbed him from behind. A vine wrapped around his leg and dragged him through the mud.

He twisted and clawed at the earth. Another tree-man jumped over the one dragging him to land with its thick legs on either side of him. Dex punched at the soft spots on the creature's legs. It released a deep sound that stunned Dex for a moment. It pounded his chest, face, and arms. Another female tree-folk wrapped her branches around his wrist and jerked his hands upward, allowing the other beast to land intense blows that sounded, to him at least, like train wheels chugging along a track. He couldn't breathe. The pounding came at a succession too fast for him to recover. The branches pulled on his arms and legs, stretching his torso like one of those torture racks in medieval times. The tension kept him still for the continued onslaught.

"Dex! No!"

A bright bluish-green explosion of dust, followed by a rumbling earthquake, shook the ground below him. The tree-man pounding him froze. Its vine-formed body became dry then brittle as it fell apart around him. The same thing happened to the others in succession. Coughing then spitting blood, Dex pushed himself up. He stumbled, pivoting to look for Yori.

"Yori! Yori!" Dex limped from one dead heap of wood to another until he got to where he'd last seen Yori. His body ached in its fight for rapid healing. The ground was covered with what appeared to be sprinkles of blue and silver dust. In one spot, it covered everything. Dex followed the trail of it, dread and fear scorching his veins. Someone had dragged Yori away.

A horn blasted behind him. He turned. A gold scepter with a red stone rose slowly from the swamp. Within minutes, it stood as tall as a staff but with a thicker base that his hand would barely be able to grasp. The stone glowed brighter as if beckoning him. Dex gritted his teeth. The decision to find Yori or to get the scepter warred in him a moment. With a grunt, he turned away from the trail of pixie dust and ran toward the scepter. It was what they had come for. Yori had sacrificed herself for this. Dex hoped it had answers.

At least, for now...the rain had stopped.

·45·

With each step he took toward the mouth of the swamp, his heart ached. The urge to run back toward the trail of Yori's remains nagged him. Dex didn't want to leave, but he pressed on. He had to get this clue to take them one step closer to the truth, a redemption—an answer to what he was, a Vigilant.

The mud grew thicker with each step, and the scepter moved further away as if taunting him to come deeper into the murky swamp. No birds chirped around him to welcome the end of the constant rains. The smell was sour like wet garbage and something else. Dex didn't stop; he kept his eyes on the red glow of the golden scepter that appeared to stay still while the water moved forward around it. Dex didn't know why it seemed like he was moving in slow motion, but with each step, it felt like he was pushing against a wall that wouldn't budge.

He wanted to look behind him to see how far he'd walked but was afraid that if he did, the beacon he was after would disappear. He rubbed his fingers against his thumbs, testing a reach for the jewel. Its gold hue turned a deep blood red and throbbed like a heartbeat, he jerked his hand back. The flash from when he'd put on the Soul Warrior ring warned him about touching the stone.

His feet were growing heavier. The mud inched up his legs with each step or movement. It wasn't something he was stepping into though. Instead, it felt like tiny hands tugging at his legs. The sensation climbed higher. It was creepy and uncomfortable, but Dex did his best to ignore it. As each tiny hand pinched at his leg, he felt a more worrisome sensation of his feet being engulfed in thick mud that made walking difficult. Dex sloshed the water around his thighs with his hands.

He was close...so close to the scepter he could almost touch it. He leaned forward and reached for it. His heart thundered in his chest. Dex's fingers closed in around the base of the staff. The base holding the gem moved. The strings of gold crisscrossed over the stone as if protecting it. The scepter vibrated. Then the red hue of the stone shuddered, changing to blue.

He released a breath. "Now what?"

The mud slithered through his legs and formed into small fingers. Dex was sorry he asked what was next. The sensation unsettled him as his feet, legs, and thighs were accosted by the feel of firm fingers within the mud around him. Brown mud pushed up through the water to cover Dex's chest and the swamp around him. Mud creatures rose from the murk with firm and well-shaped bodies that could be considered beautifully sculpted. Each was different in size and shape, but the scowled expressions they wore were the same humanlike features that seemed to mimic his face.

The first punch from a mud-man to Dex's chest felt like a rock hit him. Wind expelled from his lips, but he gripped the scepter tighter. It was the only weapon he had, but he didn't want to break it. He elbowed the creature. Part of its face crumbled at the contact. Even so, it sprang for him with groping hands clenching and unclenching. Another grabbed his shoulder and wrapped a hand around Dex's neck. Dex dug into the muddy arm, hoping it would yield like the one he'd punched. It did, but the rest of the arm hardened around his neck as its mud body grew more solid-ified. Dex twisted and dipped lower, squeezing his free hand through an opening in its hold around Dex's neck. He punched his fist up, breaking the creature's arm, and lunged forward to hit the other creature with the base of the scepter.

Blue light sparked from the stone. Instantly, the mud creature melted. In its place was a dip in the water surrounded by thick mud from the remaining creatures. Other creatures moved in. Dex slapped, kicked, and cut through them with the scepter. Each time, the creatures melted, leaving water behind.

Dex fought until his arm was spent, but he heaved and grunted until he'd destroyed every one of the mud-men and only water remained.

"What was that?" He pivoted to see the shore. He was near where he started even though he'd felt like he was in a sea of quicksand that stretched for miles.

He shook his head, facing the swamp again. He lifted the scepter, squeezing it harder in his hand.

The subtle splash from a paddle hitting the water caught his attention. Dex squinted. He focused on a dark wood boat and hooded figure that was pushing toward him. He couldn't make out a face, only the dark brown beard that framed a pale nose revealed that what neared was possibly human. Dex heaved; he wasn't interested in another fight. He dropped his shoulders, and the scepter fell to his side.

The figure came closer. Dex hoped it was someone with answers. If it wasn't someone else looking to kill him, that was. The person had gloved fingers and a black jacket that touched the tops of his black boots.

Dex stood there waiting for the boat even though his body yearned to go search for answers about Yori.

It stopped in front of him. "Get in," a deep, gruff voice demanded.

"Wait. Who are you? My friend...I lost her here." Dex flexed his fingers and bent to pick up the scepter.

"You came seeking answers to a much more important question." The man made the statement while the boat remained unnaturally still.

"Yeah, I came to find out more about the Vigilant." Dex sighed. "I need their help."

"Nothing is free or without trial. First answer, get-in-this boat, or you will never know."

Dex bit his lip and grumbled. He pivoted to take one last look behind him, his heart and mind calling to Yori. Dex prayed that she knew he'd wanted to protect her. He dropped his shoulders and got into the boat.

The man pointed to a gold contraption in the bottom of the boat. "The scepter...it goes in there and is the key to our passage."

Dex placed the scepter inside of the gold platform in the middle of the boat.

"Pull it. Don't touch the stone."

Dex tugged it closer, and the boat started to sink. Slowly, it moved in a circular motion. The mud beneath him loosened. Dex leaped into the boat. The water rose into a tubular wall that surrounded them as they sank lower to the dirt bottom of the swamp. Waves of the water moved as though a bubble of air surrounded the boat, pushing the water aside while creating a pocket for them to breathe.

The man reached over and pulled the scepter toward him.

"Whoa!"

The boat sank further beneath the mud. Worms and bones littered the mud-caked wall. How this was happening, he didn't know. What the heck was this? The glimmer of the clouds above moved further and further away as they were lowered. He was tempted to reach out and touch it, to see if he could put his hands in the dirt.

"Don't move; it'll rip your fingers off." The gruff command stopped Dex's movement.

Finally, the boat stopped descending. It now rested in a cave with only the tube of sand, water, and a minuscule glimpse of the clouds far at the top.

The man snatched the scepter out of its base. The top of the cave creaked and groaned as the rocks expanded and cracked until closed. There were several popping sounds as the torches that lined the cave lit spontaneously.

Dex couldn't stop his jaw from sagging. It was like nothing he'd ever seen, and he'd witnessed way too much in the Void.

"Shut your mouth and follow me. Answers don't come cheap."

Dex scrambled out of the boat and followed the man in black and the scepter that was no longer red, or blue, only clear and as brilliant as a diamond.

Dex wondered: Were things going to get better or much worse?

·46·

Dex followed the man without asking any of the dozens of questions tormenting his mind. The cave's tunnel bore a dampness to it, and some spots even dripped water. Torches lined the way. It wasn't cold but musky. Dex didn't like the sticky wet feeling of jeans and his shirt but was glad the backpack remained on him. He frowned, wondering if the map was any good.

They came to an open area with a domed ceiling. Various pointed rock formations with lighted tips made the room warm and inviting. Several couches were lined with fur skins and pillows of different sizes and colors, making it look like each was collected along the way and added to the frame to make it seem as though it was art itself. A desk made from tree trunks and a large wood plank that was shiny and shellacked smooth on the top sat nearby. The chair was a wood bench.

"There are clean clothes behind the curtain in the extra bedroom. Change, rest, and eat. Then we talk." The man's gruff voice echoed as he disappeared down another tunneled corridor.

Dex wanted to comment, but his head hurt. His heart was seized in his chest with loneliness so deep he couldn't stop a wayward tear from falling to mix in with the dampness on his face. He grunted, wiping his hand down his face. As strong as he was, everything here in this Void seemed stronger. What was the point of having super-human strength if every time you fought for your life, the creatures had it too?

Dex went to the curtain and opened it. Folded clothes lay on a wood shelf waiting on him. Sweatpants, a long sleeve shirt, socks, shoes, and some boxers. A towel and washcloth sat on top with a note.

Wash and change and meet in the main room.

He didn't hesitate. A metal tub sat near a wood chest next to the cot. It seemed like the guy had been expecting him. Dex swallowed down the question: how could that be?

The tub was full of cool water, but Dex didn't care. He climbed into it. He couldn't sit, though. It was too small for him. He wiped a hand down his face while thinking that Yori would have fit perfectly. He pushed his fingers against his eyelids and released silent sobs for her. He'd failed at keeping her safe.

Dex sighed and dropped his hands to his sides. Not feeling any better, but at least his grief was tucked back down deep within him—for now. Taking the toothbrush, he cleaned his teeth long and vigorously. He bent, picked up the soap, and washed his hair then his body.

Dirt skimmed on the top of the water. He stepped over the edge, hoping none stuck back on him. He dressed. His body drummed with the ache of healing he'd come to accept. Unfortunately, his heart and eyes burned with the pain of loss. He didn't know how much he could take before he'd just give up fighting.

Fully dressed, he stretched, grabbed the damp backpack, and sat with it on the bed. Movement outside of his curtain jarred his thoughts, and he decided to put the backpack under the cot. Dex crouched, placing his hands in the concealed backpack to remove the maps, their parchment was damp but held up fine. The ink seemed imbedded within the papyrus, which was what Detective Whalen called it. Dex flattened it out and put it under his pillow.

Getting up, he rolled his shoulders back and stood to his full height. Dex felt like he had no words. Yet many words crowded his mind with the anxious desire to ask more than his mouth could speak. He went to face the person who had promised him answers.

The man reclined in a large chair in the corner of the rock-walled room. Dex glanced at him, and then at the chair in front of him, next to a woodstove.

Dex fell back into the tall chair. The cushion was soft, and he welcomed the comfort.

"It's been a while since I've seen you." The man's deep voice echoed a bit in the room.

"I don't remember meeting you. Ever." Dex cleared his throat and kept an eye on the man's dark eyes, so dark they appeared black on his pale skin. The guy didn't seem much older than his father. He was thick like his dad with gray sprinkled in his brown beard.

"I first met you when you were a baby. I conducted your newborn blessing ceremony. Then...well, I brought you back to us when you were absorbed by the magic of this place."

"Absorbed by the magic?" Dex didn't want to admit to having the Soul Thief ring. He didn't remember this guy, and he had no way out of this place if things went bad.

The man nodded. "Alright, I see you aren't comfortable with your secrets. I am Jeb. One from the Vigilant counsel that trains new people who cross over."

"Cross over means what?" Dex fought the urge to rub his sweaty palms on his pants.

"Those who tap into the connection of the Creator of the multi-universe can always be free of the hold of a dark one.

This place…do you know how it came to be? Why your father brought you here?"

"I know it's called the Void and that people and their families were being lured here because of some connection they have to a Queen."

"Ah, you know some things. Well, a quick start at the beginning. This Void was a hiding place of the fallen angels. They brought their human women here and taught them about magic, science, the universe, and much more. A war happened, and they were cast within another dimension of suffering, but their children remained here. The children absorbed the magic of this place and were filled with it."

"Wait?" Dex raised a hand. "These magicals are children of fallen angels? Like the vampires, wood sprites, tree-folk, and…" He covered his sagging jaw with his hand and exhaled behind it. Blinking several times and shaking his head, he let his hand fall to his knee.

"Yes. To fast forward, the king of the Void found a way to travel from this magical realm created by the fallen angels. They'd disappeared when they were thrown into hell. He made a treaty with a powerful King from Earth that was to be sealed with the marriage of their oldest children. The daughter was highly blessed and favored, named to the line of men that had great spiritual gifts. The Earth-born daughter was named Kera. This universe, Eversphere, borders the one to Earth. The son who married the Earth-born daughter was named Cyrillus."

"Ugh. Wait, I have seen him. The guy isn't that old."

"Those born of magic don't age like you or I. Especially that one. He has made himself a god here. He is now an eternal as long as the stone of power resides in his body. He was evil born and was able to absorb an ancient stone of power. Unfortunately for him, his wife Kera was in love, but not a fool. Kera followed him when he sought to merge with the powerful source of magic. She fought him until the stone broke, distributing that power between them."

"Is she still here? Why was my family brought here?" Dex rubbed his forehead.

The man studied him a moment then ran his fingers down the side of his beard, tugging it gently before repeating the action. "She escaped through the portal, wanting to warn her family of Cyrillus' deception, but once she passed through, the Creator of the multi-verse wouldn't allow her to go home; the evil within her from the stone was too great. She prayed and begged then finally offered herself as a guardian between the portal and Earth."

Dex frowned. "If she is a guardian, why are magicals still able to get in and people able to leave?"

"A body is not proportioned to cover an entire sphere. Let me just say the portal she protects is crucial to all beings. Cyrillus needs to get to Earth to access and partner with another evil. Kera chose a specific location, which is said to be the gateway to hell, to use her body as cover—a barrier. The real reason Cyrillus and his father lured her here was to use her spiritual ability to connect to the spirit of the Most High—to use that to locate the entry to hell. They wanted to reunite with the fallen, their forefathers."

Dex couldn't speak. What Jeb shared was so unbelievable, yet what he'd seen and been through made it a dark reality. "Where do you or I fit in this?"

"Cyrillus created Soul Thieves and Trainers to act as a policing force in the Eversphere. After a while, he found other portals to Earth reported to him by those magicals that had stolen humans from there. He transformed the first human and realized it gave him easier access to the Earth

Realm since the Creator allowed them to pass easily back and forth. Provided the stone was not within them..."

Dex covered his face with his hands and leaned forward. "My father—he was a Vigilant?"

"Yes, he'd once been lured here, turned Soul Thief, then converted by one of our elders." Jeb cleared his throat. "He helped us further infiltrate, but then your sister was born, and he wanted to leave here. As for us Vigilant—we have a special gift. Where there is more than one of us, we can pray for passage through the barriers between the Void and Earth. The challenge is finding the passages. They come and go. Your father was lucky. We helped him escape, and we left him to live his life—until Cyrillus planned for war."

Dex dropped his hands. "So the Vigilant is the reason we came here? The reason my father risked all of our lives? It's because of you?"

The muscle in his chest twitched before his stomach bubbled with nausea. He'd come full circle. All he'd lost, all he'd sacrificed, and he got his answer. He didn't like it though.

He covered his face with his hands as a growl deep within him came up and out of his mouth. It didn't sound human. It sounded broken, beaten like he felt.

"Look, son."

"Don't call me that. Only one man gets to, and he is not here. He never gave me the answers I needed." Dex was angry at his father, so angry he wanted to hate him, but he couldn't, and wouldn't, give in to that feeling. He'd wanted to be like his father so many times and had failed. In that instant, though, he forgave his father. Dex had made tons of mistakes he'd wanted forgiveness from—so starting with forgiving had to be a way to get it.

"I'm sorry this has come to your head, but when our ancestors don't do what they were created to do, it falls to their children to do them one better. Your destiny brought you here. Not your father. He failed at it while trying to protect you. He felt betrayed by the Vigilant when you turned because you took the Soul Trainer's ring and put it on your hand. The moment you did that, you endangered the Vigilant's mission and call to stop Cyrillus from breaking the barrier and setting the fallen angels, now demons, free on the Earth realm."

Dex dropped his hands. "How is this my fight? I don't want any part of it. I want to save my family and get out of here. I lost the woman I'm in love with on my way here. She sacrificed herself to save me. She did it thinking I would get answers and help to fight to save them. Now you want me to do something for you?"

"You can't save one without the other. I have one request for you. If I train you to be ready, I need you to agree to free this item for me. I will be able to share with you the location of your sibling and maybe even your mother. It comes with a price, though."

Dex narrowed his eyes. There was only one person who always asked for a price. "Megan? Did she make a deal with you? If you are working for her, I don't know if your intentions are good or bad. She...something is wrong with that girl."

Jeb smirked. "She is a human and a Rumpelstiltskin descendent. Lucky for us, her human part has given her some empathy. The Vigilant have a way of deciphering a being's nature—I am particularly gifted in that area. Megan is not exactly trustworthy outside of her own desires. However, she doesn't want this war. She wants revenge on Cyrillus. Because of that, she partnered with us. She knew we were the only group powerful enough to hinder him from his purpose. For this battle, she is on our side and can be trusted."

"What does she want, and what is she giving you?" Dex crossed his arms. Part of him wanted to get as far away from Jeb as possible. He felt trapped, not by binds but by the circumstances. Jeb knew he wanted to save his family; it was the only reason he'd come this far.

"She promised to find the location of your father and sister. Once she's found them, she will bring them to me. I will reveal you and, well, the treasure. It's the only other thing that has the ability to stop Cyrillus from manipulating the magicals into war with the Earth Realm to set the demons free."

At that moment, there was no doubt he would do it. To lay eyes on his father and his sister… The sister was likely EmVee since she was the only one not in the hospital—the same as his father. Detective Whalen had made it seem like there was a way out of the Void, and that meant using the Soul Trainer ring.

"How would someone get out of here—easily?" Dex wanted to know—had to know—there was a small chance of that for his sister and father.

"The ring. The Soul Trainer ring and a human soul provides easy passage—if you know where the gates are, and that's the trick. Magicals, they can cross but usually with the use of magic to manipulation or sacrifice of a human. Nasty business it is."

"My father, he still had my ring." Dex saw his father put it in his pocket. He'd spied him with it later, and his father had tucked it in a small satchel in his office.

"So, there is a chance he got free of this place. I don't know how Megan would be able to convince him to come back. She doesn't do the dirty work. Her power is in the manipulation of people, magicals, and beings to do things for her."

Dex smirked. "Like a demon?"

Jeb raised an eyebrow. "I would suppose that most magicals here are descendants of the fallen, which in turn were considered demons. So, maybe that side of her with magic works in her favor."

"Is that the reason there aren't any churches here? I

thought that was strange when we first moved where we thought was in Newport, Rhode Island."

Jeb nodded. "It's why there are none, but the Vigilant have made their own havens for connection to the Creator. So, there is one here when you need it. But that is just a building when the real connection happens within you."

"I guess this is where I have to make a decision. I agree to train with you to be ready and to free the item you are seeking. Can you help me by giving my girlfriend a decent burial? She disappeared in the swamp, fighting the Tree-folk and I don't think she survived. I want to use your sanctuary to pray for her and, maybe, to ask that she still is alive somewhere."

Jeb stared at him a moment. "Deal."

·48·

He collapsed on the floor next to the metal tub filled with water. Dex had gotten blood on the rug, but he didn't care.

Jeb was trying to kill him. Dex knew it. Literally. He'd been stabbed, cut, shot, bitten, and smashed. The sick bastard did something to him that could have killed him. If he hadn't been enhanced, his physical life would have been over. Each time he nearly died; Jeb timed how long it took him to heal then tried to kill him again.

All those years of training to fight with his dad gave him no edge when fighting Jeb. The guy was lethal, strong, and almost seemed like he had an uncanny ability to see what was happening before it did.

Dex crawled to the tub and splashed some of the cool water over his face. "This blows. What am I doing?" He was starting to think this was a bad idea. Jeb told him he hadn't even started the official training. He was doing an 'evaluation' of his talents. Dex felt more like Jeb was using him as his personal punching bag.

He'd grown accustomed to aches, but the near-death comebacks hurt deeper than skin and muscles. It felt like it tore through his soul. Once, he'd flat-lined and felt his soul rise from his physical body to look down at his broken form. Dex was scared, really thought that was it for him. He'd felt a strong forceful hit behind him and a whisper that vibrated through his form, *not yet*. He didn't know where that voice had come from. It wasn't his. It was soft and soothing though.

That only happened once. After that moment, his body seemed to get tougher and recover at a faster pace. Problem was his heart didn't, nor did his soul. He'd thought about Yori at that moment. Dex had wondered if dying meant he would see her again.

Now, when he finally had time to think, he knew seeing her again was an impossible dream. Dex pulled himself up by the edge of the tub and the side of the cot. He dipped his foot into the water and welcomed its cool soothing. Cuts seemed to dull when water hit them. He washed, thankful for water. He had the chore of taking the buckets to the surface to fill up and dump into his tub. The worst water runs were for cleaning up some other poor person's flesh and lifeblood off the floor and walls of the training room. Since the blood was mixed with a greenish tint, he didn't know if it was human or some creature. The more days that passed, the deeper burgundy the blood turned and contained only a few sprinkles of green within it. He'd thought it was odd and asked Jeb about the color. The older guy just told him to do the job, no questions. So, Dex did, and after a while, heck, he began to look forward to it since it meant the beginning of a training session.

Today, Jeb wanted to talk to him after he got cleaned up. Since the moment they'd had the deep and revealing conversation about his father, the history of the Void and the Vigilant, Jeb barely uttered two words to Dex outside of demands. That was fine with him because he didn't have words he wanted to share with anyone. He needed time to think, fight, sulk, and decide what to do next.

He dried off, tossed the towel aside, and glanced at the grimy water littered with blood, dirt, and possibly pieces of his flesh that weren't absorbed during his healing. The wound from a sword Jeb slashed down his leg was almost completely healed with the exception of a thin scar that was slowly knitting itself to the clear brown skin that was there this morning.

Dex put on jogger pants and raised an eyebrow at the brand name *Nike*. He pulled on the long sleeve shirt while sitting on the bed. He reached under his pillow and grasped the map he studied every night. Yori had taught him some of her map memorization skills. The technique involved creating a story out of whatever you had to remember. Then, you repeated the story, over and over again, until you could recite every direction and point on the map to reveal the objects you had to memorize. He created the story he would repeat that made it easy for him to decipher the map whether he had it in his hands or not. She was embedded in his memorization story, hopping through each path on the map. Dex hoped she would be proud of his new skill. He regretted he didn't bother to seriously develop it until he'd lost her.

He used the finger on his free hand to trace the outer shape of the map. Then, he closed his eyes and visualized it in its entirety, using his artistic skill to picture it as a 3D image in his mind. The tiny vision of Yori appeared to follow the path. The back of the map within the parchment had additional hidden clues when held up to the light. Dex twirled the map around in his mind then opened his eyes and lifted it in his hands. He lifted it up to the light and noticed on the back there was a hidden image that represented a glowing box bearing strange symbols. Dex squinted at the design then closed his eyes to etch the newly revealed clue to his story and his picture.

There was movement on the other side of the curtain, so

he slid the map back under his pillow. He put on the tennis shoes Jeb had given him; it was his eighth pair since he'd been there. The days and nights were slipping by quickly and painfully.

"Dexter?"

He frowned at Jeb calling him by his full name. The man never listened when he told him to call him Dex. "Coming."

Dex came out into the main room. Jeb stood there, changed into loose black pants, black shirt, and black cloth shoes. Dex wondered why the guy never wore a different color. Maybe because black doesn't show blood as easily.

Jeb gestured toward the large steel table surrounded by wooden chairs. The makeshift kitchen was in the room next to this one and had a dug-in oven and firepit. Dex knew because it was his job to make breakfast for them, and he'd made bread in the oven and eggs over the fire.

"I caught us a rabbit and picked some of the carrots you liked for the stew. The bread's good; you've got a skill for making it."

Dex sat down and sighed. "Thanks, it relaxes me and gives me something to beat on."

Jeb chuckled, then sat, prayed over his food, and grabbed a spoon. "I've got good news."

Dex stopped his spoon before it touched his mouth. Then he swallowed. "What is it?"

"Megan informed me that she can make good on her exchange. That means she has located your father and possibly your sister."

"When can I see them?"

Jeb played with his beard. Dex held his breath, knowing the movement was Jeb thinking—or holding back information.

"You are almost there, son, but not ready for what we

need you to be prepared to do. That means doubling my efforts. I need you ready in two weeks. We have to get the item, and no one knows where it is. Megan is trying to get a clue, something to point us in the right direction. She eluded to the capture of a valuable creature the Soul Trainers created then let escape. That creature may know how and where this item is since he was one of the main guardians of its hiding place."

"I don't understand. How long have I been here? Since my father left?"

Jeb's dark eyes captured Dex's. "Time is relative here. However, if you must know, your father's been missing about a year."

Suddenly, Dex wasn't hungry. He dropped his spoon and closed his eyes. So much had happened, but he never had been able to keep track of the time lost. A year since his siblings had been captured, tortured, and lost to him. He was going to be sick.

·49·

I t had been a long two weeks. Dex put his gloves on his hands. They were leather, or something like leather, similar to the rest of the suit Jeb left for him to wear. He didn't know what the new outfit meant, or why his typical sweatpants or joggers weren't sufficient for him to practice in, but Dex didn't care. He liked the new clothes, a lot, too much.

Even though his body had been hit hard, he felt like he'd grown through it. Dex had recovered and rebuilt a part of himself that captivity had taken away. He put the map in his backpack he'd tucked away. He put the backpack on and made his way to the library Jeb had shown him when his training began. It was where Dex spent time studying more material than he'd ever remembered consuming in any school. From scrolls to ancient texts about the Void written by the Vigilant elders, informants, and loved ones who were magicals.

Jeb was bent over a scroll on a long wooden table in the center of the room. The shelves and drawers of materials he'd collected were neatly tucked away in their proper place. Jeb was picky about that. Dex's ear twitched from the many times the man had grabbed it to remind him to put the books and scrolls back where they belonged.

"I'm ready." Dex stood at the doorway.

"Come in. I am deciphering the information Megan sent."

Dex hopped on the balls of his feet then walked over. The picture was a cube with cryptic writings on it and a glow. The etchings were similar to the ones that he'd seen on the notes written by Detective Whalen's wife. Dex knew he'd seen it before.

"What is it?" Dex swallowed.

"A lock. There are clues to getting to the location, but we need to know how to find this lock and decipher it to set the item free."

"When are we doing this?" Dex studied him while he wondered if telling him what he knew mattered at this moment.

"Now. There is only a brief time that the guards change and there are fewer of them. We have a good team that can take them down, but I don't want to cause too much of a ruckus. We have to do this quietly, and the Soul Warriors are good—real good—at what they do."

"I'm ready."

Jeb stopped studying the design on the table and stood to his full height, which had to be about 6'7" since Dex still had to look up to him a bit.

Jeb nodded. "Yes, you are ready. I am proud of the progress you made. You surprised me, but then again, you come from a line of strength."

"You told me you would tell me the secret to up my abilities when I needed to."

"True. To up it, connect with your creator, ask Him for the help, but hold on, you never know what form it will come from." Jeb played with his beard. "Let's make our way to the surface. First, though, we have to make a stop."

Jeb folded the paper that was on the table and tucked it into this jacket. Of course the jacket was black as was the rest of his outfit. Not as form-fitting as Dex's and made of a cloth material that didn't resemble the leather Dex wore, but Dex sensed it wasn't cloth. That it was firmer and likely didn't rip.

Dex followed Jeb through the many tunnel corridors and put them to memory, wondering if, after this journey to meet the conditions of Megan's trade, Jeb would ever return.

The burnt stone cavern was beautiful and rustic. Dex had appreciated each area that was revealed to him as though it was art. Even the training area that he had to clean off blood each morning before his session started with Jeb was well designed from the natural flow and veins in the rocks. He'd wondered who had cleaned his carnage from the training floor when he'd been too broken to do it himself. Even so, every morning, bluish-red blood was splattered on the floor and the walls of the cavern. Jeb made him clean it up, and Dex did without complaint.

Torches were already lit in each tunnel. This made Dex wonder if they were alone. He hadn't met or seen anyone but Jeb the entire time he'd been in this place. There was the exception of a creature or two that Jeb had him fight off during training. Even so, at times, things seemed to be taken care of, or prepared, while he slept or been out of the room.

They came upon a stairwell carved into the brownish-red stone. A man Dex didn't recognize stood there. He was dark-skinned with thick muscles and a goatee sprinkled with black and gray hairs. His head was bald and his eyes a startling grey. If Dex were still in New York, he would joke that the guy was wearing colored contact lenses, but he could tell the dark man's eyes were real.

"Meet Moaz. He will take you to meet your partner, give you time to get acquainted, then bring you both to the surface."

Dex frowned. He wanted to ask about this *partner*. "Teacher, I don't think I'll need a partner."

Jeb's lips thinned. "I made you a deal, right? You promised to follow my direction and training, give your life to meet the conditions to see your family, did you not?"

"Yes." Dex exhaled, he'd realized he'd slipped in his training. The part about trusting elders. "I'm sorry. My promise is true."

Jeb nodded and pivoted away.

"Dexter Lewis...you resemble your father." Moaz pulled him into a hug.

"Ugh!" Dex shook his head and pulled away. "What the..."

"Sorry, I haven't seen you since you were a baby. I'm your godfather and far removed cousin."

Dex frowned. "My father never said..."

"He couldn't once he left here with your mother and your sister the first time. The Vigilant can only stay safe if no one knows their names. The smaller the footprint we leave, the better. I paid passage to visit when you were born. Sadly, I wasn't able to visit when the twins came."

"I see. How did you become a Vigilant?" Dex walked alongside him.

"I fell in love with a beautiful Soul Trainer, but the Soul Thief turning her was in love with her. She, uh, was in love with him too but thought playing with my heart was fun. So, to be with her I had to be one of them, and I did. My brother saved me, dying in the process."

"Your brother died? Was he one too?"

"No, he was a Vigilant and gave up his cover to save my stupid ass." Moaz punched the side of the cave wall as if still punishing himself for his mistakes.

"I'm sorry. I am the reason my family was discovered too.

I should've never taken the ring from my friend's dead body, but I didn't know what it was and wanted to give it to his sister—my old girlfriend."

"Hmm, luckily Jeb got to you before your soul was lost and your DNA altered beyond repair."

"So, there is a point of no return?" Dex rubbed the back of his neck, thinking about the darkness and emptiness he'd felt when he put on the ring of a Soul Thief.

"Yes. When the human part of you is altered by the magic beyond repair." Several wooden doors signaled the end of the tunnel. Moaz turned to face Dex.

"This is it?" Dex tilted his head to see around Moaz.

"It is. Your partner is in there. They've given up a lot to be here, basically cut away a part of themselves to walk in the footsteps of the Vigilant. One of the most painful transformations to be Vigilant is for someone who was born a magical and denies that part of themself to allow their human side to dominate. The transformation to Vigilant is like death to an old version of themself and life to a part of themself considered weak—until they realize the true source of the Vigilant's power is beyond understanding."

"I won't be a prick to them. I'm not like that." Dex stood, pushing back his shoulders.

"Good. I put a lot of work into this recruit, and as you cleaned their blood, they cleaned yours. It's a bond that partners in the Vigilant have, becoming one body, moving with the same accord, starts with being humble—being able to care."

"I'm ready," Dex assured him by patting his arm and bowing his head a bit as he had for his teacher, Jeb.

Moaz smiled. "You be the teacher. This one has only one last hurdle, and that's the one of loss."

Dex knew what loss was. He could help them get

through it. He wasn't over his loss, but he made the pain of it give him focus and keep him grounded.

Moaz left quietly. Dex stood in front of the door. All he had was to open it and say the words Jeb told him to say to his partner in the Vigilant to seal both of their places in the Vigilant book of warriors.

·50·

Dex opened the door, expecting to see a brother in arms. Instead, the small stature of a female's back faced him. Her dark hair was wavy with curls; a hood hung just under its length. Form-fitting black pants and sturdy yet stylish boots came up to her knees. She was studying a fight plan nailed to the wall. The intricate drawing of coordinated moves by the straw men on the parchment bore an artful style.

Jeb had taught him this and acted as the partner in a loosely choreographed dance of coordination that would make him a dangerous competitor. Dex had drawn his fight plan on the floor in chalk. Each morning, he erased it to redraw it again like Yori had taught him.

The girl placed her hand on her hip. Dex's heart nearly stopped in his chest as she slowly turned around to the closing door.

"Teacher?" Her voice was soft and tentative.

Dex's hand came up to his chest. He couldn't move to take a step. A lump formed in his throat at the sound of the husky voice he'd dreamed about every night. He couldn't help the tear that fell from his eye as he soaked up the beauty in the form of the young woman he'd fallen in love with, and failed to save.

"Dex? Dexter!" Yori's voice broke as she ran to him. Her face had changed. The silver tattoo that had grown with her use of magic was gone. Her brown eyes were no longer trimmed in lashes of bluish brown. She appeared much more human and less mystical than she had before. Even so, she was astoundingly beautiful. The change was a more fiercely confident stance, straight shoulders, and sexy saunter of that of a warrior.

Dex snapped out of his daze and widened his stance to catch her as she ran, then jumped, into his arms.

"Love...Yori." He broke down and buried his face in the crook of her neck. Dex held her to him so close. Her scent was different yet just as intoxicating. Tears soaked his shoulder from her sobs.

Dex shuddered. He remembered the deal he'd made with Jeb. His eyes were closed. He inhaled Yori's scent. Jeb had given him a quiet ceremony to put Yori to rest. He'd remembered Jeb saying, *we are dead to our former selves and live in the new.* Dex had wondered at the meaning. Jeb's promise was more than met since Dex had never hoped to see, much less touch, Yori again.

He gently set her down. Dex couldn't let her go and so placed his hands on her shoulders. Yori's beautiful eyes blinked up at him. Her stature was sure and strong, yet her hand shivered, wiping a tear from her cheek.

"I didn't know you made it."

"I thought you died." Dex sniffed and rubbed his thumb on her shoulder.

"A part of me did, and it needed to go. It was holding me back." Yori grasped his hand and tugged him over to the small loveseat near the fireplace.

"You have a nice room." Dex smiled, realizing he may have been in this room if Moaz hadn't found Yori. Jeb put him in one of the main rooms to separate them.

"My teacher graduated me to this room after I took the vow to become Vigilant."

Dex sat next to her and placed an arm around her shoulders. "Was Moaz your teacher?"

"Yes, his brother helped sometimes by carrying me to my room when I couldn't move."

Dex frowned. "His brother?"

"Elder Jeb."

Dex raised an eyebrow. "But Jeb is..."

"Jeb looks Caucasian, but he is Moaz' half-brother. They have different moms." Yori giggled. "I asked. He was shocked since I don't think they are used to many nosey females around here."

"What happened to you during the fight with the Treefolk?" Dex released the breath he'd been holding. He couldn't take his eyes off Yori. She had changed, seemed to be overflowing with the strength he'd seen inside her all along.

Her eyelashes fluttered, but she forced her back to straighten. "I let the magic in me take over when I saw that they were attacking you in droves. I couldn't let what happened to you with the diseased shifters happen again. But before the magic could come back within me, a Treefolk strangled me. I lost consciousness."

Dex took her hand, the one that was balled up in her lap. Every other feature on her seemed calm as she unfolded what happened. Dex held back his desire to squeeze her in his arms. Her breath caught occasionally, letting Dex know this was hard to share. "How did you survive?"

"The cocoon. My body seems to sprout one if I am near death, then it repairs me."

Dex frowned, studying her. "You look different."

Yori smiled and put a hand to her hair then her face. "The blue hairs and silver magic marks, they are gone because of me crossing over to the Vigilant. The magic in me diminished, and the human in me was able to grow."

"So you don't have the power to do magic?" Dex rubbed her back.

"Not magic in the sense that I would have before. I have the ability to use the power when given from the Creator of our humanity. It's different, not based on what I want but what I am granted when needed."

"Are you okay with that?"

She laughed. "I am more than okay with it. I feel free. Magic, and use of it, comes with a price. A bit of your soul, or someone else's blood, comes with it. I no longer have to pay that price."

"I'm happy and feel the same. How do you feel about being my partner?"

"I am glad it's you. I'm ready to make the vow."

"So am I, but I am taking out the old language and bringing it up to date. You know?"

"Oh, yes, I was thinking the same thing."

Dex placed her hands within his. "*I, the Vigilant, will take the care of my new sister in arms. I will fight to the death, tho, there will be life everlasting. I vow to protect, to care for, and to never leave behind one of the chosen. I promise, as a knight of the Vigilant, to defend human life, value second chances, and be obedient to that inner spirit which guides me.*"

Dex closed his eyes as Yori repeated the vow, feeling the tinge of electricity between them before sealing their vow with a kiss.

·51·

There was a knock at the door. Dex turned his gaze away from the fight plan Yori had drawn. She moved next to him.

Jeb and Moaz carried dark leather bags looped on each arm. Weapons sprouted out from the opening of each pouch.

"Deal met." Jeb tossed Dex a dagger.

Dex caught it and put it in the strap under his arm. "You more than met it. Why didn't you tell me she was still alive?"

Jeb's eyebrow rose. "I didn't know if she was. All I knew was Moaz found a cocoon washed up onshore. He coaxed her out of it and wanted to see if he could help her."

"Thanks, Moaz." Dex went to shake the big guy's hand but got pulled into a bear hug.

"It's what I do, try to save people. Half-breeds deserve a second chance. They are part human and deserve to know about the gift of being so."

"I don't know what would have happened to me if he didn't save me, if I hadn't become a Vigilant," Yori said. "The darkness of the magic was addictive."

"Eh! Whenever there is an easy way out of things, people take it." Moaz chuckled and handed her a few knives. "Here's your favorite." He extracted a sword from the bag. It was in a leather casing that had an elaborate design on it.

Yori squealed. "Oh, teacher! It's the best gift ever. Thank you!" She gave him a hug.

"You earned it with blood, sweat, and tears. You are ready."

Jeb's face turned serious, and Dex couldn't help the reflex to drop his smile and pay attention.

Jeb cleared his throat. "We will meet the other Vigilant warriors at the access point. The only problem is no one knows where to find the cube. It's a lock, and until we know how to release it, this may be for nothing."

Dex bit his lip. He remembered his map. "I know where the cube is. The map we got from Detective Whalen has the location. We didn't think we needed it at first."

Yori stepped forward. "Yes, he insisted we take it. He made sure we didn't leave without it."

"We can take you to it." Dex stepped over to the corner where he'd dropped the backpack and dug inside for the parchment. "Here it is."

Jeb grasped the maps. "Don't you need this as a reference?"

"No, I spent every night memorizing it."

Yori smiled. "You learned?"

"I did. I was too stubborn to notice it was just as important as all the other crap we dealt with."

"Good, I will take this then. We will meet the others. If I give this to Megan, she may back off her other demand."

"Wait? What other demand?"

Jeb's jaw tightened. "She wants me to use my friendship with an insider to get the location of the ones called Sandmen."

"What's that?" Yori tightened her belt around the sword's handle.

"It's men, or magicals, that are held near death by Cyrillus and their souls used to manipulate the dreams of others. Sometimes, they can be made into visions and drive awake men to madness."

"How would we even find Cyrillus?" Dex followed Jeb and Moaz out of the room and into the tunnel.

"When we find the treasure we've been looking for, he will be able to lead us to Cyrillus," Jeb grumbled. "The informant Megan sent to retrieve it made mistakes, and it sacrificed itself for her life. Megan works with juveniles, kids easy to manipulate, and they are impulsive – making serious mistakes."

"Did you plan on finding this treasure and then freeing it?"

"Yes, it was lured here by an evil Soul Trainer named Sybil. Then she tried to trap it. One of Megan's apprentices freed it by accident, but it sacrificed itself so the apprentice could get free. It was a mess," Jeb spat. "She should've never sent a child to do her dirty work."

"Isn't that the way Megan operates? Use others, make deals, and get what she wants?"

"Sure, but we don't have to like it. Besides, even Megan can change; she is part human." Moaz pushed open the wooden door.

Dex counted the steps. "How many stairs are there?"

"Too many." Yori laughed. "Moaz made me run these every day for water to clean the training rooms."

Dex's heart twanged. The days he'd cleaned up blood off the floor, it had been hers. "Jeb, why didn't you make me go on that errand?"

Jeb grunted. "It was her job, and she preferred to wash and heal in the hot springs."

"Hot springs? I missed out."

"Not if you decide to stay after all of this," Moaz said. "So, hurry up or we will be late."

Dex took the steps two at a time. He was looking forward to seeing what the rest of the Vigilant looked like. If they were old or young. But the one Vigilant he'd be forever grateful laying eyes on was, and always would be, his partner Yori.

·52·

It's seemed like forever since Dex had seen daylight. It wasn't as brilliantly sunny as he remembered, but he didn't mind a cloudy day. The teasing taste of water hung in the air with the richness of vegetation. The woods had moments of thick cover that opened up to green and flowered patches that seemed like mirages in a long path of dying leaves and draping greenery.

They'd walked for miles while Jeb and Moaz rode horses. Dex inhaled once more. The horse had another underlying odor that was human. It was a shifter, not just horse. The trail they traveled was thick but had hidden paths that only Jeb and Moaz moved through with ease.

"We switch now," Jeb directed.

Yori climbed onto one horse, and Dex pulled himself onto the other.

"How much further?" Dex tugged the horse's mane, and the creature looked back at him, dipping its eyebrow in annoyance.

"Pesha knows the way. Just ride," Jeb muttered. "There, over the small hill, they wait for us."

The horse, Pesha, was sure-footed and moved with a sleekness and boredom the made Dex feel as though the horse wanted him to get down. Instead, he relaxed and went with the flow of her pace.

Jeb had gone over the hill. Pesha stopped and bucked her hind up. "Okay, you want me off? I got it."

Dex jumped down at the same time as Yori. The trees were spread out. What little there was of the sun above the clouds when they'd left had set. At least the woods were dry and the clouds gone. The moon was bright, casting a light glow on the meadow of grass with a border of closely tangled trees.

His mouth dropped. So many Vigilant warriors crowded the meadow. All ages, colors, and faces. None of them mattered as much as the girl of thick curly auburn hair. A tanned skinned guy had his arm around her. She was his sister, and she'd returned.

Dex's legs moved quickly; he outstretched his arms. "EmVee! You came back!"

She ran to him and hugged him. Her embrace was stronger than he remembered. EmVee had changed; she smelled of wolf with equal amounts of human.

He pushed her back slightly. "You're here?"

EmVee smiled up at him. "You've grown even taller than me." She sniffed. "And smell like a leopard."

"You smell like wolf."

Her eyes narrowed. "We both have changed—but inside here—" she tapped his heart—"we are still the same."

"We are."

"You're a Vigilant?"

"Yeah. You?" Dex's gaze bounced behind her to Kayson. Dex didn't know if Kayson knew the details of his father's death.

"We are."

Kayson walked up to him. "I took care of her like you asked."

"Thanks. Your father..."

He raised a hand. "I know he was framed and killed."

"I'm sorry." His chest shuddered. He'd never forget the image of Detective Whalen's sacrifice.

"We all have something to be sorry about. Now, let's focus on changing it." Kayson grasped EmVee's hand. "It's time to talk to Jeb."

EmVee placed a hand on Dex's cheek. "I have a surprise for you." She moved away.

There was a break in the group. A tall, light-skinned black woman with red hair laced with gray walked toward him. Her arms and legs muscled and toned from years of boxing and training. His mother smiled at him.

Dex couldn't move. He'd never considered seeing her again. He'd thought she died in the crash.

"Dexter, my son." Tears fell freely from her eyes. "I knew you would grow, of course, but you are a young man now. I am so happy to see you. I'm proud of who you've become."

Jeb walked toward them. Dex's mom stepped aside.

She embraced him. "You saved my son and made him ready. Thank you."

"Mom, this is Yori – my girlfriend, partner. She saved me more times than I can count."

His mom smiled at Yori and gave her a hug. "Thank you for being there for him."

Jeb nodded. "Now we must hurry. He knows where the key is, and his partner has the tools to open it. We need to create a diversion once we get beyond the walls of the barrier. Can you take half the team and do that?"

"Of course. My husband, he's...we have to save him. Cyrillus turned him into a Sandman."

Dex frowned. That meant his father was being held and near death.

Jeb cursed. "He could give away all our secrets, everything he knows about the Vigilant."

"He would never do that." His mother placed her hands on her hips.

"Then his soul could be held that way forever, eternity, suspended in the hell Cyrillus creates for him."

"We will save him and my other children."

Jeb sighed. "Yes, we will, but not at the risk of the mission: stop Cyrillus from accessing the power to kill the barrier between him and our home."

"It will fall in place." His mother touched Jeb's arm.

Jeb turned to Dex. "You and Yori sneak in while the others create a distraction. Unlock the key and bring the treasure out."

Dex shook his head. "What is the treasure?"

"An angel, one not of the fallen. He still holds his light."

Dex swallowed and hoped he wouldn't screw this up.

·53·

Dex led Yori through the thick vines and branches covering the entrance to the hidden ancient underground city.

Yori climbed up and over Dex, whispering while she pointed, "Orion's Gate is used by magicals to go undetected by humans living here. It is believed to have a secret portal to all the Provinces. The Provinces are governed and separated by species of magicals like vampires, shifter nations, werewolves, faeries, mermaids, succubus, and even more. The Warlords over this Province are supposed to control the others that are deployed to the other Provinces."

"There are guards everywhere." Dex looked down into the valley. There was a wall made of gray rock and cement that spanned maybe half a mile. It was cracked, worn, and had spots of decay. Several guards stood at each entrance—men tall and muscled who stood stone still. Huge statues of thick men bore the faces of beasts. Muted glowing outlined the structure with encased rocks that held up weak sections of the wall.

"Those are statues of berserkers, men cursed with faces of beasts and hearts of men." Yori nudged him with her elbow. "But right there—" she pointed—"is our way in when they give the call."

Dex allowed his gaze to travel the wall. He knew exactly where they had to go. So many of the guards protected the outer perimeter of the underground city. He didn't know how they would get belowground where the treasure resided. Even in the darkness, his keen eye caught an unusual movement. A boy around his age was walking on top of the wall. Dex narrowed his focus and realized the kid had silver-hair. Dex swallowed. There was only one other creature he'd known with hair that color, and it wasn't someone he'd wanted to run into again.

"I can't believe this," Dex muttered.

"What?"

"Nash is here."

Yori inhaled a shaky breath. "Oh my God, no. He will ruin this for us."

"I thought Jeb said someone working with the Vigilant would be waiting here. Someone who would give us a diversion."

"He did."

"Where are they?" Dex had a sinking feeling that Nash was the 'they,' but he would wait to make judgment.

"I don't know, but we have to do it tonight. It's the only night of a full moon that will unlock the cube that is used to lock the treasure within."

Dex thinned his lips at Nash who, with a flick of his wrist, extracted a flute.

"C'mon." Dex wanted to be able to slip in if he could. He kept low to the ground with Yori right on his heels.

"We need to make our own diversion." She moved in front of him.

"Yeah, in order though. Don't rush it. Be patient." Dex remembered the warning like a second voice in his head; it was what Jeb drilled into him every time he made a mistake in haste.

Dex crouched low. Yori slid next to him like a shadow. It amazed him how Jeb and Moaz could teach each of them, without putting them together, how to be so in sync. He moved low and silent toward the wall. The leopard blood in him made it easy to see in the dark and almost sense where to step for sure-footedness. Something fluttered behind him. He didn't turn to see what it was but knew Yori stuck to his every move.

Nash filled the air with a tune. It seemed to weave out of the flute with a glittering magical hue. The sound skipped over the top of the wall, down around, then into the ears of the massive beastly statues that were hunched in front with weapons. The Soul Trainers moved side to side as though bored but stayed on watch. They suspected nothing until the sound from Nash's whistle broke the air.

His song flowed as though from an unknown instrument as it seductively reached inside its listener's thoughts. It stunned a few of the guards, but many seemed alerted by the change in the others and scanned around them.

"Now!" Dex leaped from the overhanging hill. The statues moved. A thundering of falling rock pounded through the air as the wall broke away where they lunged from their crouched war stance. They punched upward as if fighting themselves awake from a long sleep. The guards who must've had their ears covered—protected from Nash's song—jumped into action.

Nash leaped from the wall and onto a guard frozen by his song. His tongue whipped out and into the neck of the victim. Another guard charged at him, and Nash released the weakened victim to toot a tune. One of the living statues grabbed the guard from behind, crushing him until his body went limp. Nash jumped onto the towering statue's shoulder to break the neck of the guard. The beastly statues and guards fought. Clashing of weapons, yells from the fallen brought more guards into the battle.

Dex ran toward the entrance that was littered with guards fighting statues. He zigzagged between them, breathing a sigh of relief they hadn't noticed them.

A sharp whistle called behind him. Dex stopped, pivoted, and stared into the green eyes of Nash.

"You thought you could set me up and run?"

Dex swallowed. "I didn't."

"Liar! You took her from me. Yet you promised I could have her if I helped you escape."

Dex wouldn't give in. Instead, he tried to divert him. "Why are you here?"

"Doing the bidding of my sister so I can get the one thing I asked her for in return."

"Sister?" Yori stepped up next to Dex.

"It's complicated." Nash spit a fleshy piece of blue blood from his mouth. "She let me live for a favor. Then, I let her live for a favor. We fight, but now we are family."

"Nash, I didn't set you up. I wanted to get free with you, but I didn't trust you wouldn't hurt Yori."

Nash narrowed his eyes. He whistled sharply as a guard lunged an attack at him. He sidestepped, and the guard fell into the rock hammer of one of the statues.

Yori's sharp elbow jabbed his side.

"You bartered for my life?!" Yori hit Dex at the base of his neck.

"It's not like that. You were in the cocoon."

"I can't believe..." Yori muttered.

"Nash, please let us go. A lot of lives are depending on us getting through."

"I will since this is a promise. Mark my words; this isn't over. She will be mine."

"Hello! I am standing right here."

"Sorry, let's go while we got the chance," Dex whispered, hoping she heard him.

"You bet this isn't over." Yori left him to make a break through the fighting guards.

Dex followed, feeling the heat from Nash's eyes every step of the way.

·54·

The tunnel wasn't a safer bet for them, Dex realized, as a surge of guards stampeded toward them.

"Fight them off!" Dex charged but used the curvature of the tunnel to gain leverage. He kicked the first Soul Thief in the chest, knocking him back. Another sliced the air with a blue-lined sword.

"He's got magic on the sword!" Yori yelled.

Wings sprouted from her back, and she flew over Dex's head, thrusting her sword forward. White light shot from her sword to clash with the attacker's weapons, diffusing their blue magical hue. She struck them down with her sword doused with white light.

Dex kicked one. Then another fell from a rope engulfed in light Yori had yoked around the Soul Thief's neck.

"Fight fair!" Yori growled as a guard lifted a scepter topped with a blue stone.

Dex leaped over her. He snatched the scepter from the guard's hand and smashed it against the forehead of another.

"Behind you!" Dex called at Yori who had her legs wrapped around the neck of a guard while her fist pummeled at the Soul Thief's eyes.

Yori's wings fluttered, and she flipped upward, releasing the guard who collided with the other Soul Thief who attempted an attack.

"I'm clearing the way! Follow me." She whipped out her sword and laced it with the light from within her.

Dex followed, stabbing and kicking through the felled bodies of those she'd injured with her sword. He jumped, kicked one, landed on the head of another, and ducked then punched the next attacker.

Yori blocked the entrance of the next tunnel. Dex ran toward her, thankful for the break in fighting.

As soon as he ran past her, Yori muttered a prayer fervently, over and over again. She raised her hands, and a burst of light burst from her chest, creating a barrier of glowing light that mutated to a wall of moving energy.

Dex stepped toward it.

"Don't touch it," Yori whispered.

"Is it magic?" Dex frowned and stepped back.

"No, it's from the Creator, the part that resides within me. It holds the power of creation, not that of manufactured magic. I don't control it."

"Wow, I don't think that could come from me." Dex pivoted to assess where they were.

"You have your own gifts, and I have mine. But you never know. Our gifts can change when needed." Yori shrugged.

"This way." Dex pointed to the break in the tunnel.

Yori fell in step with him. The echo of their breathing seemed to bounce off the walls.

"Almost to the location. Watch for markings on the wall. Jeb told me to tell you to touch them." Dex searched around. The tunnel was dim; the torches weren't lit.

"First, we need light. I can't see a thing. How are you able to?"

"The leopard bites improved my sight, remember? I can see in the dark."

"Good." Yori lifted her hand and blew into it. The torches all along the tunnel lit in unison.

"Creating fire now?"

She smiled. "Not me. Remember, we are given what is needed."

He led the way into the tunnel. It should have led directly to the door that held the treasure. The light flickered.

"It's here." Dex caught the glow of the suspended cube with the slashes of symbols on it. It floated but remained at the same height and twisted slowly as if on an axis.

"Creepy that no one is here protecting it." Yori stopped then touched Dex's arm. "There are ink spots growing on the path."

Dex sniffed. "Smells rotten."

Yori's hand tightened on his forearm. "Something is sprouting from them."

The hair on his neck stood on end. Kids of various ages and sizes rose from the black ink-like substance on the floor of the tunnel. As they grew to full size, the dark mass beneath them was absorbed into their skin. Their skin was pale with a grayish hue. The one closest to them had blond hair with a pallor that hung to its ragged and unkempt ends.

"Vampires? But these are different." Yori gulped.

"Like vampires but I don't know..." Dex sniffed. "Not undead. They smell like they are alive, but dying."

"Now I know why no one was here."

"We have to fight through them." Dex took a step closer.

"I'll go high up." Yori's wings flickered from her back, and she rose into the air.

One of the children sank back down into an ink puddle. Dex frowned as the others crawled toward him.

Yori pointed. "I think I have one following me."

261

One dark puddle had moved up the wall. Dex lifted his sword and attacked one as it lunged at him. Its fingers had sharp and pointed nails. He stabbed at it, and the child's black pupils dilated. A screech sounded from the others as they gained speed and came at him.

Dex stabbed another then spun around to chop off the head of one that just missed his arm. He kicked one that sprang from a puddle on the ground.

"There are too many!"

A dozen or more snatched at her wings. Their hands ripped at her, and she sliced off the offending attacks. Dex sliced off the arm of a creature that leaped from the wall.

One bit him, followed by another. As soon as his teeth released from their flesh, they burst into flames, but that didn't stop more from coming. He straightened his stance and punched one, stabbed another, back-kicked another that dropped from the ceiling.

"Do your light!"

The tunnel was flooding with them. Dex didn't know how long they could fight them off.

Yori's chanted prayer echoed like a replay on her lips. Louder and louder she got until she screamed. Light flooded the tunnel.

The fully formed creatures were instantly incinerated. The remaining dark puddles scattered, sinking into the pores of the rock to disappear.

Dex fell back against the wall, his heart racing with adrenaline. He inhaled deeply and slowly as he fought to calm his breathing. Yori flickered her colorful wings and landed in front of him. Light illuminated from her center, slowly dimming as she approached.

"Beautiful," he whispered before she tugged him into a passionate kiss.

The cube wasn't budging. It had stopped pivoting on the invisible axis when the tunnel flooded with light. It hovered as though it was on high alert of something. Dex moved his thumb over it in the order Jeb mentioned may work. Jeb never made any promises that the method would unlock it.

"We don't have much time," Yori whispered. "We have to go back the way we came. I don't know how long the barrier will hold."

"I know, but this isn't working, and it is burning my fingers. I probably won't have any fingerprints after this."

Yori giggled. "You heal instantly, so you are stuck with your fingerprints."

Dex exhaled and ran a hand through his curly mass of hair. "You want to try?"

She smiled. "I thought you'd never ask." Yori leaned in, studying the design, then bent down and looked under it. She went to touch it, and blue light reached up to zap her finger. She jumped back. "Oh no." She blew at it. "Dark magic."

Dex grabbed her hand. A black dot seemed to expand into vines around her finger.

"Your light, use your light."

Her lower lip trembled. "I can't. It's calling out the darkness in me and suppressing my light."

"What fuels it? Your light?"

"Faith. I thought...it was enough."

"It is. Let me." Dex pulled her to him and slid his hands into her hair. He rested his cheek on her forehead and chanted the Vigilant healing prayer.

A shock of power throbbed through Dex then into and around Yori. She shivered and stepped back.

Dampness from tears covered her cheeks. "Thank you, Dex." Yori glanced at the cube. "I can't touch that again."

Dex nodded. His heart beat rapidly within him. "Light up your sword. Pour everything you have into it. When I tell you, slice through it."

Noise from pounding feet vibrated through the tunnels.

Dex grabbed the cube. Blue streaks of magic shot out of the inscriptions. The pain of it seared his skin. The blood of the Vigilant and his healing power counteracted the digging in of the dark magic. Dex tossed the cube into the air.

"Now!"

Yori's sword, now covered in light, slashed downward, slicing the cube in half. Blue shards exploded from the cube as it disintegrated. The resounding energy threw Yori and Dex against opposite walls.

The once-closed end of the tunnel flickered to reveal a guy wearing an unearthly glow. He sat cross-legged on the ground.

"You did it? I had my doubts."

His glow was brilliant, light brown skin and golden curls with dimples. The guy was well built but with an allure that was unworldly.

"I thought angels had wings." Dex crossed his arms.

"I do. I'm just not a show-off."

"Um, we need to get out of here. The guards are coming." Yori tugged at Dex's arm.

"Not a problem since you destroyed the lock. I am free, and so are my abilities. You have to come closer though."

Dex and Yori allowed him to embrace them. His light grew and enveloped them. Brilliant wings sprang from his back, and in a flash, the three of them disappeared.

·55·

Dex couldn't believe they were in the main room of the hidden Vigilant training camp where he'd spent months preparing for saving this treasure.

"Why did you bring us here?" Yori paced. "And you!" She pointed at Dex. "What's that about you giving me to Nash?"

Dex put up his palms. "It was when you were in the cocoon. I didn't know what or who you were. He asked if he could have what was in the cocoon. I agreed because he tricked me."

She narrowed her eyes. "Still."

"I'm sorry, but I never meant to let you go with him. I worked hard to get him to ignore you and focus on me."

Yori sighed. "I don't know."

"Trust me, I love you and have for a long time. I didn't know what Nash was at the time, but I had to make it appear as though we were working toward the same things for him to help me."

"Your actions prove you were honest, but I don't..."

"Don't start doubting your gut feelings. You know who I am. I am more than your partner in the Vigilant. I want to be your forever partner."

Yori teared up. "I want that too."

"Good, now you." Dex pivoted to point at the angel. "Take us back!" Dex stared at the treasure they'd freed, the angel. His light was dim, and he seemed almost normal.

The guy smiled as if watching a wayward child. "There is no need to return."

"We need to help them fight!"

"They received the signal and are on the way back to their hideouts. All are safe. None of the wounded was left behind."

"How do you know that?" Dex pointed at him. "Do you have a name?"

"Afriel is my name. I know because I can see a lot more than the average person when I am transporting."

"Are you a fallen angel? Like the ones that created this place from magic?" Yori walked around him, inspecting everything about him.

"No, they are not my kind. I came here thinking I was saving someone I'd fallen in love with, only to be trapped and used for science experimentation. Until I was set free."

The pounding of feet thundered from the outer hall. Jeb pushed into the room along with Dex's sister, mother, and Kayson.

"You got him?" Jeb smiled and clapped his hands. "I knew you would."

"We did. Now what? Is Megan going to tell us where my younger brother and sister are? My father? Is she coming to collect?"

EmVee crossed her arms. "She will, but she doesn't know where this place is, so we have to take him to her."

Dex frowned. "Why?"

"We need her." EmVee sighed. "And she...needs us."

"How can we trust her?"

"She has her ways," Kayson added, putting an arm around EmVee.

"We need a plan to protect ourselves." Dex flexed his fingers.

His sister grinned wide and winked at him. That look he knew well, and he liked it.

"Oh, we have one. Her name is Rachel." EmVee smiled.

Dex laughed for the first time in what seemed like forever.

---

*D*ex and Yori were alone in the main room with a warm fire at the woodstove. She was cuddled in his lap on the couch. He never wanted to let her go. He kissed the top of her head.

"Do you think Nash was really helping us?" Yori squeezed his waist.

"Yes, in the only way he knows how." Dex exhaled. "But if Megan is his sister and thinks she can control him, she's wrong."

Yori shrugged. "I don't think so. He wants love like anyone else. We shouldn't be afraid."

"No, we shouldn't."

"I don't know if I want to leave here when we are done. There are so many things we could do to help the people here. The Vigilant has done so for eons."

"We could stay or go. Whatever happens, I am never leaving you."

Yori pulled him down to kiss her. "And I am never leaving you."

A fullness and a peace he hadn't felt in a long time invaded his heart. With Yori by his side, finding his father and his younger siblings was possible. Anything was with her belief in him—in them.

THE END

Read Rei's story in Break the Darkness,
coming November 2020.

Please review Novel at By LM Preston
www.lmpreston.com\store

Please support LM Preston by leaving reviews at your favorite retailer.
LM Preston: www.lmpreston.com
Blog: http://lmpreston.blogspot.com/
Tweet Me: http://twitter.com/LM_Preston

A NOTE FROM THE AUTHOR

Thank you for reading Scepter of Fire, book 2 of the Vigilant Series.

If you have enjoyed it, please consider leaving a review. You can visit my book page:

Scepter of Fire
www.amazon.com/gp/product/B07XVS23LG/

Don't forget to sign up to *LM Preston's Newsletter!*
https://landing.mailerlite.com/webforms/landing/v6q7e4

DISCOVER THE NEXT BY LM PRESTON

Don't miss the next book in the series due out November 2020!

BREAK THE DARKNESS,
Vigilant Book 2.5

Rei was nosey. She'd been told it would always get her in trouble, but it never did. Until she met Megan, who promised her the job of a lifetime. Sure, the high school newspaper wasn't the ideal job for most, but for Rei, it was a dream. She'd never considered putting her investigative nature to work, but what Megan asked her to do was way beyond the requirements of a school newspaper. It was part of an underground news-for-favor service. Rei's partners, Asher and Eli, annoyed her by never trusting her to do a job alone. Maybe this one time she should have listened, because being trapped with no one to bail her out will mean her death. Not only hers. She would be forced to spill the secrets about her family she'd been withholding, placing every one of them in grave and serious danger.

Pick up the other copies within the series:
Insatiable Darkness Book 0
Caged Fire Book 1
Unbreakable Darkness Book 1.5
Scepter of Fire Book 2

OTHER BOOKS BY LM. PRESTON

The Pack by LM Preston–

Teen, blind, vigilante on a mission to save the missing kids on mars. Shamira is considered an outcast by most, but little do they know that she is on a mission. Kids on Mars are disappearing, but Shamira decides to use the criminals' most unlikely weapons against them—the very kids who they have captured. In order to succeed, she is forced to trust another, something she is afraid to do. However, Valens, her connection to the underworld of her enemy, proves to be a useful ally. Time is slipping, and so is her control on the power that resides within her. But in order to save her brother's life, she is willing to risk it all.

Bandits by LM Preston –

Daniel's father has gotten himself killed and left another mess for Daniel to clean up. To save his world from destruction, he must fight off his father's killers while discovering a way to save his world. He wants to go it alone, but his cousin and his best friend's sister, Jade insists on tagging along. Jade is off limits to him, but she insist on changing his mind. He hasn't decided if loving her is worth the beating he'll get from her brother in order to have her. Retrieving the treasure is his only choice. But in order to get it, Daniel must choose to either walk in his father's footsteps or to re-invent himself into the one to save his world.

Wastelands – Bandits Series, by LM Preston – Daniel's doing the unthinkable. He's planning to break into a prison to prove to his dead father that he has changed, only problem is – he hasn't.

Flutter Of Luv by LM Preston–

Dawn, the neighborhood tomboy, is happy to be her best friend's shadow. Acceptance comes from playing football after school with the guys on the block while hiding safely behind her glasses, braces, and boyish ways. But Tony moves in, becomes the star running back on her school's football team, and changes her world and her view of herself forever.

Explorer X-Beta by LM Preston –

Barely escaping their captors, Aadi and Eirena are determined to save their dying friend. After their final confrontation with the species that tortured them, they've changed— unfortunately, not for the better. The changes caused by a terrible experiment force Aadi to accept the possibility that he may never be fit to go home, and that holding onto his sanity, or leading his friends to safety will end in failure and may rip his friendship with Eirena apart, forever. Time is slipping away and the possibility of losing his friend is not an option, but the foe that awaits them may be worse than the one they left.

Insatiable Darkness –Book 0 - Prequel to Caged Fire Book 1: Vigilant Series—

EmVee didn't know what to think about this new town her father's passion for boxing lured them. It was an unlikely location for her to pursue her dream of going semi-pro. Just when she started getting used to the school with gorgeous jocks and strange cheerleaders, the depth of the danger her father's choices dangled them in front of became clear. EmVee hoped Silas and Kayson will be able to help her uncover the mystery identity of the person who is threatening her family. The question is, will she survive to expose the mystery.

Caged Fire - Book 1 - The Vigilant Series—

They say you can't run away from your problems. EmVee knew from experience it was true. She and her father tried to run, until the truth came and got them. Now with nothing to lose, she must confront the monster that changed her life forever. Unfortunately, she has to work with his best friend, Kayson whom she is almost sure isn't quite as nice as he seems. Kayson revealed not just why her father disappeared, but a new world of magicals that wanted the debt he left behind to be paid. (Insatiable Darkness - Book 0, Caged Fire - Book 1, Unbreakable Darkness book 1.5)

Unbreakable Darkness –Book 1.5 - Prequel to Scepter of Fire Book 2: Vigilant Series—

Dexter never looked for trouble, it finds him. Moving to a small city from New York wasn't his idea of an improvement. His plans to make his dreams of being groomed as a pro football running back ended the moment his father uprooted his family. Day one, he landed in jail without bail and realized too late that his father made a deal to get him out, one that would change his life, and put his family forever in danger. Unfortunately, finding love always happens at the worst possible time. Dexter didn't realize that love could also kill. Again, trouble, it finds him, but this time he'd face it – head on, and hope he survives. Prequel to Scepter of Fire Book 2 in The Vigilant Series.

Scepter of Fire –Book 2: Vigilant Series

Dexter didn't like being a pawn. It seems life was taking him there though. His father and he never saw eye to eye, but being captured and tortured for his father's mistakes gave Dexter too much to think about. First, the girl he lost, he'd never forget what they did to her. It changed him and made him see the small city his father moved him to for what is was, a prison for magicals, the damned, and now him. Too bad, the creator of the void didn't realize they would be better off if they'd set him free because now, he was fighting for his life and someone he'd have to hide his feelings from to protect, not just from those who want to drag them back but from him -a vigilant.

ABOUT THE AUTHOR

LM. Preston is an avid reader. She loved to create poetry and short stories as a young girl. With a thirst for knowledge she attended college and worked in the IT field as a Techie and Educator for over sixteen years. She started writing science fiction under the encouragement of her husband who was a Sci-Fi buff and her four kids. Her first published novel, Explorer X - Alpha was the beginning of her obsessive desire to write and create stories of young people who overcome unbelievable odds. She loves to write while on the porch, watching her kids play, or when she is traveling, which is another passion that encouraged her writing.

For more information, please visit
www.lmpreston.com